5

SEAL'S HARMONY: A PROTECTOR ROMANCE

RED FALCON 1

LYNNE ST. JAMES

SEAL's Harmony

Published by Coffee Bean Press
Edited by Rebecca Hodgkins
Cover by Lori Jackson Designs
Created in the United States

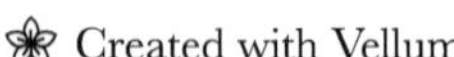
Created with Vellum

DEDICATION

For all the spouses and families who are patiently waiting for their soldiers to return home.
As always, for T.S., my real-life hero. I love you!

ABOUT THE BOOK

SEAL's Harmony is the kick-off to the Red Falcon Team introduced in SEAL's Angel.

The first time Navy SEAL Ryder "Ry" Purcell sees Harmony Taylor, he's rushing to her rescue as she's about to fall into his friend's wedding cake. Ry soon finds himself smitten by this accident-prone beauty. But issues from his past still linger, and he doesn't know how far he's willing to take things.

Bank manager Harmony Taylor is used to falling, but not so hard or fast as she has for Ry Purcell. Half the time she wonders if it's the man or his dog that she's crazy about. Since she grew up with a controlling father, the sexy SEAL's alpha tendencies make her wary. But when Ry rescues her from a scary situation at the bank, she sees him in a whole new light.

Ry is positive that Harmony is in more danger than she believes, and it's escalating. He brings in the members of his Red Falcon team, but will it be too late to save the woman who has stolen his heart?

1

Navy SEAL Ryder "Ry" Purcell took a swig of his beer and checked the time, hoping his teammates wouldn't notice. Weddings weren't his thing. Though as weddings went, this one wasn't too bad. Rafe Buchanan and Meghan Henley's ceremony on Virginia Beach had been short and sweet. One he might like for himself if he ever went down that road someday far in the future. He'd planned to skip the reception and just wander down the shoreline with Whiskey, his German shepherd teammate and constant companion. Basically, walk off into the proverbial sunset and no one would be the wiser.

It had been the perfect plan until Cam Patterson, the K-9 handler on the Black Eagle team, suggested they let their dogs burn off some steam before taking them inside for the reception.

Ry had agreed, even though it meant he'd lost his window of opportunity to make his escape. The reception had been going on for over an hour, and he was ready to get the hell out of there. It's not that he was antisocial, but his team just finished a mission and got home yesterday.

After spending the last month cooped up with these guys, he was ready for some alone time chilling at home. Instead, he was sitting at a table with all of them, nursing his second beer, and listening to his teammate Luca "Lucky" Rossi going on about his countless conquests.

Zoning out, Ry tilted his chair onto its two back legs and gazed up through the glass solarium ceiling. A cerulean blue sky dotted with puffy white clouds floated overhead and reminded him of the opening sequence of the Simpsons. For a moment the music and buzz of conversation disappeared, and he was somewhere far away.

"Hey, Ry, could you at least try to seem like you're having fun? Your grimace is frightening the women away," Quinn Gallagher said. He was the leader of the Red Falcon team.

Quinn's voice pulled him right back into the noisy room and ended his virtual escape. Ry leaned his elbows on the table and shrugged his shoulders.

"Yeah, what's your problem? Free booze. All you can eat food. Single women. What more could you want?" Josh Hartman, another one of his teammates asked.

"Seriously? You're telling me you wouldn't rather be on the couch in your civies with a beer and your feet up watching the game? Or at the Ready Room? Fuck. Anywhere, as long as we're not in our dress whites." Ry sighed. He sure as hell would. Getting dressed up and sitting around was not his idea of a good time.

"Are you worried about catching the bouquet?" Lucky laughed and waggled his eyebrows. He was the team clown and could make them laugh even under the worst conditions.

"Men don't catch the bouquet. It's the garter, you idiot. But I'm keeping my happy ass right here when it happens."

With the way his luck had been going today, he'd probably be the sorry loser to catch the damn thing.

"You're being such a pansy-ass, I figured you'd get up there with the single women." Lucky smirked and tossed a wadded-up napkin at him.

"Go piss up a tree, Lucky. If it's so much fun, why are we all sitting at this table instead of out there with all the single women? It's not just me at this table." Ry lifted his beer in a salute then took a long swig and finished the bottle.

"I guess you schooled us, huh?" Quinn chuckled. "But you have a point. We're not in high school hiding from the girls. Time to stop moping and have some fun. These are our friends. The least we can do is get our asses up and mingle." His gaze met Ry's. "And no sneaking out before they cut the cake, or you'll have extra PT for a month."

"Got it, boss. Whiskey and I won't leave the building. You don't have to worry about us."

Quinn tipped his chin in acknowledgment, and after a brief look at each of the men, he headed toward the bride and groom.

Ry eyed Whiskey as he rested his head on his knee. "I guess I need to mingle. You need to stay here, bud. I promise I'll bring you back something good."

The dog made a low woof and laid down with his head on his front paws.

"You heard the boss, you guys coming or what?" Ry chuckled as Fergus "Doc" O'Brien flipped him the bird.

"What I want to know is how did the Black Eagle team have time to find their women?" Josh asked.

"Seriously, bro. They got sent on all the good missions and found them, rescued two of them. I think Knox likes them better than us," Lucky replied.

"I don't know about that," Ry said. But maybe Lucky

had a point. Their missions were in Africa dealing with Boca Haram and rescuing kidnapped schoolgirls. Not exactly dating material.

"Rafe didn't meet Meghan on a mission. He met her at Norfolk Airport on his way to see his sister. You need to just chill. Keep your eyes open, ya bums. You never know what will happen," Doc added.

"You mean it's like Mom used to say? 'You'll find the perfect woman when you're not looking for her.'" Lucky smirked.

Doc pushed back from the table and straightened his uniform. "Why not? If you're not open to anything, you won't find jack shit."

"I guess it can't hurt to mingle a bit." Josh finished his beer and got up. "You fuckers coming or what?"

"Yeah, I'm coming, bro," Lucky said.

"If anyone is going to find a woman today, it'll be you, Lucky." Josh rolled his eyes as his friend slid his hand through his wavy black hair.

"Stick with me and I'll show you how it's done."

Ry shook his head. Josh was right about the attraction thing. If there was a woman within a three-hundred-foot radius, Luca got lucky. He'd earned his nickname on one of their first deployments. But he also was a love 'em and leave 'em kind of guy. Some thought that made him lucky, too, but Ry wasn't so sure.

"Whiskey, stay. Be good." Ry leaned down to ruffle the dog behind his ears. Then he made his way across the room to grab another beer from the open bar. Beer in hand, he stood at the edge of the dance floor and stifled a yawn.

"Not getting enough sleep?" Tony Knox, the commander of the Black Eagles and Red Falcons, asked before taking a drink from his glass.

"Sir," Ry responded, and stood at attention. Since he was in his dress whites, it seemed appropriate.

"At ease, Ry, it's a wedding." Tony slapped him on the back.

"Some habits are hard to break." But apparently not being aware of his surroundings at all times, since Tony had snuck up on him.

"It turned out great, didn't it? I'm glad we got Rafe back in time."

"Yeah, me too. Wait, what?" Ry's team returned yesterday from the mission they took to keep the Black Eagles home for the wedding. "They went on a mission?"

Tony took a sip of his drink before answering. "Something came up that had to be handled."

"That sucks, but I'm glad he made it back. Meghan was probably a wreck." Ry looked over to the head table, where Quinn and the newlyweds were laughing. He liked Meghan, and he'd never seen Rafe happier.

"Yes, but they know the deal, and so do their women." Tony tipped his chin toward the girlfriends of the Black Eagles where they were talking to the DJ. "Some of them were *the* mission. I'm sure seeing their men in action gave them a different perspective."

"That's for damn sure. But not all women experience what we do. Thank God for that. What kind of world would that be?" Ry hoped he'd settle down someday, but he also knew that being in special ops took a toll on a relationship. When he committed to a woman, she'd be his everything. Same as it was with his parents.

"Everything okay?" Tony asked.

"Of course. Why wouldn't it be?" It was an odd question coming from his CO, especially since he had debriefed them yesterday.

"You look like you'd rather be anywhere than here."

"Wouldn't you? No offense to Rafe and Meghan. But I'd much rather be relaxing than all dressed up and bored out of my mind."

"You could ask the blonde to dance who's been checking you out for the last five minutes." Tony tilted his head to the right.

Tony wasn't wrong. Ry looked in the direction he indicated and sure enough, two women were watching them. When they caught his eye, they giggled. "I don't remember seeing them before. I'd remember them if they'd been to any of the team BBQs. Do they look familiar to you?"

"No, but I don't hang out with you guys. It is a wedding though, they're probably friends of Meghan's from Atlanta."

It looked like they were trying to get up the nerve to come over. If there was ever a time when he wanted to be invisible, this was it. Ry would take armed tangos any day of the week over women who chased men in uniforms.

"If they head this way, I'm going to disappear. Just warning you," Ry said.

Tony smirked. "What? A frogman afraid of a couple of mermaids?"

"You got that right. They aren't mermaids, they're sirens in disguise, ready to suck the life out of you first chance they get."

"Whoa. Who pissed in your beer? When did you become such a cynic?"

"I'm not, just a realist. I've been around my share of women who are only interested in the uniform and the paycheck." Ry sighed. "Okay, maybe I am a bit cynical."

He just wanted to find someone who didn't look at him like he was a choice piece of meat or wanted bragging rights for fucking a SEAL. But the longer he looked, the less likely it became.

"There is someone for everyone. Jake even found someone perfect for him. If Dawn hadn't come along, I'm not sure he'd have gotten out of the hospital alive," Tony said, his gaze on the couple as they danced with her children.

"That's true."

Tony chuckled. "Looks like the blondes finally worked up the courage to come talk to you."

"Maybe they want to talk to you?"

"Highly doubtful. I'm ancient, look at all my gray hair. Trust me. They don't want any of this." Tony gestured down his body.

"Maybe they're into silver foxes?"

It must have hit his funny bone, because as soon as the words left his mouth, Tony lost it. The guffaw that came out of his mouth took Ry by surprise, and most of the other guests turned in their direction. Ry couldn't remember if he'd ever seen his CO laugh like that.

"Thanks for that, but I'm pretty sure they're coming for you."

"Shit, I guess it's too late to make a run for it." Ry took a swig of his beer, straightened his shoulders, and prayed for a distraction. As the two blondes made their way over, he glanced at Whiskey. If the dog made one move toward anyone, he'd have a reason to excuse himself.

Tony elbowed him in the side, and Ry pasted a smile on his face as the women stopped in front of them.

"Hi, I'm Shelley and this is my sister Sharon. We're friends of Meghan's from back home." Blonde number one flashed an overbright smile.

"Nice to meet you. I'm Ryder and this is Tony." Tony had been right. They weren't from around there. He tried to catch Lucky's attention where he stood by the buffet table, but the man flat-out ignored him. The douche canoe knew he needed to be rescued, but winked at him instead.

"Do you work with Rafe, too? We met some of his other teammates earlier," blonde number two asked.

"I'm not on his team, but I do work with him sometimes. Tony is the boss of both teams," Ry explained.

"Oh, really?" blonde number one said and batted her eyelashes at Tony. "You're the boss man, hmm? Is it hard telling all these gorgeous men what to do all day?"

It took all Ry had not to burst out laughing at the look on Tony's face. Even if he paid for it with extra PT, it would definitely be worth it.

"And what do you do?" blonde number two asked.

"I'm a dog trainer," Ry said. It took a lot of effort to keep a straight face at the look of disappointment on number two. He'd bet a hundred bucks that she was cursing her sister for getting the boss when she got stuck with the dog trainer.

"I guess that can be exciting," she mumbled, and moved closer to her sister.

Ry would have to remember to use that line in the future if he needed an escape. Th bigger surprise was how well Tony handled small talk. Maybe Ry would ask him for some pointers for the future.

"Ry, why don't you tell Sharon about Whiskey?" Tony suggested.

"What about whiskey?" blonde number two asked.

"Not a what, a who. Whiskey is my dog." Ry pointed to where Whiskey had been lying halfway under the table. But he wasn't anymore. He was on all-fours, with his ears cocked forward. Something had him agitated. "If you'll excuse me, I need to check on him."

Ry didn't wait for their answer and set off across the room, trying to figure out what triggered his reaction.

Unable to figure out what was going on, he had to wait until he made it closer to Whiskey to see the problem.

A petite blonde looked like she'd lost her balance and grabbed the table to keep herself upright. Except the table wasn't steady, and it looked like both the woman and the wedding cake were about to hit the floor. Before Ry could do anything to stop the impending disaster, Whiskey reached her side, grabbed the bottom hem of her dress, and pulled her away from the table.

The scene unfolded in slow motion as Ry got there just in time to catch her as she lost her footing. He scooped her up into his arms as Whiskey whined next to him.

"What just happened?" the woman asked as she blinked up at him.

The violet eyes gazing up at him took his breath away. It was a moment before he answered. "My dog rescued you and the wedding cake from certain disaster. I just kept you from hitting the floor. Are you okay?"

"I think so. Umm, can you put me down?"

"Oh yeah, of course." Ry lowered her to the floor. When he looked down, one heel had broken off her shoe. "I think you might need a new pair of shoes."

"What? Darn. I just bought these, too. That'll teach me to wear high heels."

Ry bent over to pick up the heel. "Are you here for the Buchanan wedding? I don't remember seeing you earlier. Do you want me to get anyone for you?" What the fuck was wrong with him? He was rambling on like a teenager.

"No, no one. I'm really fine and yes, I'm supposed to be here. It just took me a while to decide if I was going to come or not." Her cheeks flooded with color, making her eyes look even more purple. Then she looked away from him and kicked off her shoes. They both bent to pick them up at the same time, and only Ry's quick reaction kept them from banging their heads together.

"I guess staying home would have been the smarter choice," she said and ducked her head to avoid his gaze.

Before Ry could ask her name, Chrissy Stillwell grabbed the woman's arm. Chrissy was Meghan's best friend, Ryan McLaughlin's fiancée, and a CIA operative. But the coolest thing about her was she had an eidetic memory. The woman could unravel any plot she uncovered, and there had been plenty.

"Holy fuck, girl, are you okay? When I looked over, I thought I saw you come in, but then you disappeared. Did you faint? Why was Ry holding you?"

2

"No, I didn't faint. I'm fine, except for almost taking out the cake. If they hadn't come to the rescue, I'd have taken it out. Crisis averted."

Harmony looked around, hoping no one had noticed the near disaster. She could see the headline now: "Drunk guest takes out wedding cake, news at eleven." Thank God they'd saved the cake from her. She knew better than to wear four-inch heels. Buying them had been her first mistake, but the saleswoman's pitch had sold her, and they looked great with her dress—or did before she broke off the heel.

Five minutes. Five blessed minutes. That's all it took for her to embarrass herself in front of one of the most gorgeous men she'd ever seen. One who didn't live on the covers of her romance novels.

Chrissy laughed. "I guess you weren't kidding when you said you're a klutz?"

"Why on earth would anyone joke about that? It's mortifying. Seriously," Harmony answered before turning to her tall savior with chestnut brown hair. His eyes crinkled at the corners as he smiled at her. But she couldn't tell if they were blue or green. "Thank you so much for coming to my rescue." Harmony reached out her hand, palm side up, to let the handsome German shepherd sniff her before she scratched him behind the ears. "You are a noble steed. Thank you for saving the day."

The large dog woofed and licked her hand.

"His name is Whiskey, and I'm Ryder—Ry, actually. I hope he didn't hurt you when he pulled you away from the table."

"Nothing but my ego and my shoe and both were my fault. I'm indebted to you. I shouldn't be surprised since this is a room full of heroes. Thank goodness you saved the cake, or I'd be on the next plane to the North Pole to hide. Oh, and I'm Harmony Taylor, it's very nice to meet you." She'd said all of that without stopping to take a breath.

Ry laughed, really laughed, not some forced one like she was used to getting from Herb. The deep sound resonated within Harmony, filling her with warmth. Embarrassing herself was nothing new, and she used humor to hide her mortification. But he was different. He didn't make her feel clumsy or stupid.

Though if they gave her another five minutes, she'd probably fall flat on her face. It was the story of her life. Harmony was the only person she knew who could trip over air. She'd be upright one minute and flat on her face the next. High school had been a living hell.

"I don't think you'd have to go that far, maybe just the next county?" Ry's smile lit up his entire face. Like he needed to be any more magnificent. He was addling her brains, and she'd just met him.

"You're both being ridiculous. C'mon, Harmony, I know Meghan will be happy you're here. We figured you were going to ditch on us." Chrissy steered Harmony toward the front of the room, nearest the beach. Even with the glass doors shut, Harmony could hear the roar of the waves as they washed up on the beach. It was the perfect backdrop for the wedding.

"I should have ditched. Everyone would be safer. Who knows what calamity I'll cause next?"

Chrissy giggled. "Girl, you are not that bad. You didn't fall once when we were at the bank."

"Just lucky, I guess," Harmony murmured as they made their way across the room. "Was that one of Rafe's teammates?"

"Who, Ry?" Chrissy looked over her shoulder. "Nope, he's on a different team, but he works with Rafe sometimes. Why?"

"Just curious. He has some serious moves and is very easy on the eyes." Harmony was dying to see if he was watching as she walked away, but she held onto her last bit of pride.

"He's a good guy, not like Lucky. His name and number are on the stalls in the girls' bathroom at the Ready Room. Call for a no-strings-attached evening." Chrissy grinned.

"You're kidding, right?" Harmony didn't know whether to believe her. She was pretty gullible, as well as clumsy.

"Yes, I'm kidding. But I shouldn't be. He's definitely a player, so unless you are looking for that I'd say away from him." Chrissy pointed to a black-haired man at the buffet talking to a couple of tall blondes.

"Is everyone at this wedding a model or something? I feel like Cinderella at the ball, except my fairy godmother skimped on my gown."

"You're too funny. C'mon, let's get you a drink."

"Nope, not a good idea. I'm not staying long." Harmony muttered as Chrissy dragged her over to the bar.

"Two champagnes please."

Before she had much of a chance to object, Harmony was holding her heels in one hand and a glass of champagne in the other, and praying that she didn't end up on her ass.

She hadn't even heard Ry approach and almost spilled her champagne all over them when he put his hand on her elbow.

"You startled me." With every minute she was there, Harmony's desire to run for it grew stronger. What had she been thinking? She barely knew Chrissy and Meghan. Disaster hovered over her like a rain cloud.

"How about I take those for you? I can put them by my seat, so you don't have to carry them around," Ry offered.

Harmony hesitated for about a half-second, then handed him the shoes. Maybe she could get through the rest of the evening without hurting herself or anyone else. If she played it safe. "Thank you. I appreciate it."

Their fingers touched as he took the shoes, and electricity zinged up her arm. Her gaze darted to his and from his expression, he must have felt it, too.

"No problem. Whiskey, stay with Harmony." At Ry's words, the dog sat and leaned his body against her. He probably expected her to fall over again. Though that was less likely without her shoes, it couldn't be ruled out completely.

Harmony rubbed the dog behind the ears as she watched Ry head over to his table. He'd turned her insides into mush and all he'd done was brush her hand as he took the shoes. If he ever kissed her, she'd probably spontaneously combust. Not that it would ever happen. Men like him didn't date women like her.

"He likes you." Chrissy grinned and elbowed Harmony in the side.

"He's just being nice."

"Yes, he's nice, but that's not what it is. I've known him for a while now. He's showing all the signs that he's interested."

"What? You're crazy. No way." Just thinking that Ry could be even a little interested sent heat flooding into her cheeks. "He's just being protective. Probably like the old saying, 'when you save someone, you're responsible for them.'"

"Sure, you tell yourself that, girl. He's going to ask for your phone number."

"No way. Unless he's just trying to be nice. But if you want a real bet, then I'll take it up a notch. He has to ask for my number *and* call me."

"You got it. What are we going to bet?" Chrissy asked.

"How about dinner? Whoever wins gets to pick the place," Harmony said.

"It's a bet. We have to shake on it."

"What are you two up to?" Ry asked as he returned to Harmony's side.

Chrissy gave her a knowing wink. And Harmony's cheeks got even hotter.

"I bet her that she won't have any more accidents while she's here," Chrissy said.

"You'd be correct in that assumption. Me and Whiskey will make sure of it."

"Oh, no, you don't have to, Ry. I can take care of myself." As the words left her mouth, Harmony said a little prayer that she was right.

"We want to, right, boy?"

"Woof."

Chrissy smirked. "C'mon. Let's talk to Meghan and Rafe while they're not surrounded by a ton of people."

"See, you're learning." Large groups intimidated her,

especially when she was already uncomfortable in her surroundings.

"Don't worry, we've got your six," Ry whispered into her ear.

"Thank you. But wouldn't you rather be hanging out with your friends than babysitting an accident waiting to happen?"

"I'm exactly where I want to be."

True to his word, Ry stayed by Harmony's side while she chatted with Meghan and Rafe, and then Chrissy introduced her to the rest of the bridal party. She'd heard all about Miranda, Sky, and Dawn, and how they had girls' nights when the guys were out on missions. Chrissy had invited her to the last few, but Harmony had declined, saying she was busy with work and getting settled in her new place.

When the DJ announced it was time to throw the bouquet, Chrissy convinced her to join the group of single women. Harmony held her breath as the bouquet sailed through the air and straight toward her. The other women jostled for position, but she didn't move from her spot. So the last thing she expected was for the flowers to drop right into her hands. But even better, she didn't knock anyone else out and stayed upright through everything.

"Holy crap. I can't believe I caught it."

"Things are about to get interesting," Chrissy murmured.

"What do you mean?" Harmony tried to read Chrissy's expression. It was the first time Ry had left her side to give them a chance to talk.

"They're about to do the garter toss."

"So?"

"I bet Ry makes sure he catches it."

"I don't understand. Why would that matter?" Harmony asked.

"If he catches it, he'll get to put it on you since you caught the bouquet."

"Oh no. I'd forgotten about that." Maybe he wouldn't be the one to catch it. "He wouldn't want to do that. He's just being polite, hanging around making sure I don't take myself or anyone else out."

"Girl, no man is *that* polite. Even his dog knows." Chrissy nodded toward where the two of them were watching her.

"It's kind of weird, or maybe intense. I don't need to be protected like I'm glass. I fall on my ass daily and I haven't broken yet."

"These guys are all Alpha males. You're never going to convince them they don't need to protect you. I saved Ryan's ass, and he still watches over me like a mother hen. Have you seen how he keeps checking to see where I am? It's how they all are."

"I don't know if I could handle that, no matter how attractive and nice he is. Especially after my ex had to control my every move. It's one reason I left him in Iowa."

"I'm not trying to scare you. Just explain."

"Well, I'm sure it won't matter. I'll probably never see Ry again after today."

"Time will tell," Chrissy said as she pulled Meghan out of the way while the guys gathered in the center of the dance floor for the garter toss.

Sure enough, Ry was in the middle of the group, and apparently, his friends were giving him a hard time about it. Harmony only had a moment to wonder what that was about before the garter flew right into Ry's hands.

"I told you." Chrissy smirked.

"Ugh. Maybe he'll give me a pass. And we can skip that part."

"I'm sure he will if you ask him. He'd never force you to do something if you're not comfortable," Chrissy said.

Harmony didn't have to worry. Ry and Whiskey headed toward where she stood with Chrissy, and there was no sign of the garter.

"Nice bouquet," Ry said as he stopped by her side.

"It really is. I should probably head home and put them in water."

"You can't go yet. They're about to cut the cake. There is no denying the cake." Ry's eyebrows lifted, and he looked shocked that she'd even consider skipping out on the cake.

"But it's just cake." Harmony wanted to escape more than she needed the extra calories that would go right to her hips.

"That's sacrilege. There is no *just cake*."

"I suppose you agree?" Harmony asked the dog, who was sitting at her feet with his tongue hanging out.

"It's delicious," Chrissy added. "I helped Meghan pick it out since Rafe was away on a mission."

Harmony shook her head and smiled. She'd arrived late. She probably shouldn't leave before they cut the cake. At least they still had one to cut, thanks to her new canine friend. "Okay, I give up. Cake it is."

Chrissy was right. Harmony sat with Ry and a bunch of his teammates and chatted as they ate. It was probably the best cake Harmony had ever eaten, even if she would groan when she stepped on the scale in the morning.

"What are you thinking about so hard?"

"Nothing, just cake and calories."

"But it was so good. I'm thinking of having another slice."

"Go for it. None for me, but I bet Whiskey will be happy to help you finish anything you can't."

Ry chuckled. "That's for sure. He is not picky about food. He's had to rough it as much as we have."

"I didn't think about that. But you're probably the best boy, aren't you?" Harmony said as she scratched him under his ears.

"He is. He's saved us all more than once."

Harmony's stomach twisted just thinking about the danger they encountered on missions. She didn't know how Meghan and the others dealt with the worry. Not that she'd ever be in their shoes. As much as she'd enjoyed her time with Ry and the other guys from the Red Falcon team, it was time to go. Hopefully without making a scene like she had when she arrived.

"Can I have my shoes? I'm going to head home."

"Already?" Ry asked.

Doc laughed. He'd been sitting next to Ry while they were all chatting. Then he laughed harder when Ry gave him the middle finger. If she hadn't been watching, she would have missed it.

"Yeah, I have some work to do."

"On a Saturday evening? I thought you worked at the bank?"

"I do, but I'm trying to help one of my customers. He's having a hard time and I'm trying to figure out a way to get underwriting to approve a loan for him. Anyway. It's been wonderful meeting you. Thank you, both of you, for your help."

"I'll walk you out to make sure you're okay."

Harmony didn't have the heart to say no, especially

since she figured she'd never see him again. Might as well enjoy her time with him while it lasted.

After saying goodbye to everyone, they walked out to the parking lot, and she slipped her shoes on while leaning on Ry. More little shocks of electricity zinged through her. It was probably a good thing she'd never see him again. He'd be easy to fall for, except for his bossiness.

When they reached her car, she unlocked it and turned to thank him. Ry had other ideas. He pulled her into his arms and kissed her. His lips were firm as they slanted against hers with just enough pressure to curl her toes. Without thinking, she brought her hands up to rest against his firm chest.

Then it was over.

Harmony took a step backward and almost fell against the car, but Ry's hands steadied her.

"I really enjoyed today, Harmony. I'd like to see you again. Would that be okay?"

Chrissy had been right. Or he was just being nice. The real test would be if she saw him again.

"I had a much better time than I expected. Mostly because of you and Whiskey."

"Can I have your number? Or how about you add yours to my phone, and I'll add mine to yours?" Ry handed her his phone, and she dug hers out of her purse and gave it to him.

"Okay, Ryder Purcell. And you too, Whiskey. Take care and thank you again for saving my butt and the cake."

"My pleasure, Harmony Taylor."

As she drove away with a wave out the window, she already missed the sexy SEAL and his dog. Would he call? Could he be the hero she'd been waiting her entire life for? Time would tell.

3

Five weeks later…

Ry pulled into the bank lot and found a spot near the entrance. After shutting off the ignition of his 1996 cherry red Ford Ranger pickup, he looked over at Whiskey, who was sitting in the passenger seat with his head hanging out of the window, enjoying the fresh air. The Red Falcon team had just returned from a month-long mission, and he'd come straight from the de-briefing to see the woman he hadn't been able to get out of his head.

"Do you think Harmony will remember us?"

The dog tilted his head to the side like he was considering the question and woofed.

"I don't know. It's been over a month since Rafe and Meghan's wedding." Ry ran his fingers through his shaggy chestnut-brown hair. It was one of his tells when anger or worry rode him. "I bet she thinks I blew her off. It's been weeks since I told her I'd be in touch. If she'd said she'd call or text but didn't after all this time, I'd figure she was just blowing smoke up my ass."

Whiskey whimpered and put his front paw on Ry's arm where it rested on the console between the faded cloth-covered seats. Then he leaned over and licked Ry's face.

"Thanks, bud." Ry rubbed Whiskey behind his ears. As he glimpsed himself in the rearview mirror, he shuddered. *Bigfoot anyone?* Would she even recognize him? He didn't remotely resemble the clean-shaven man she met in dress whites. It wouldn't surprise him if the bank security guard took one look at him and tossed him out on his ass.

From the moment Ry had kept Harmony from knocking over Rafe and Meghan's wedding cake, she'd lived in his thoughts. There was something so sweet and innocent about the woman. Maybe it was her self-deprecating humor, or that she could barely make it across a room without falling on her ass or causing some kind of calamity. He grinned just thinking about the near-disasters at the wedding.

"Maybe I should go home and get cleaned up first and come back tomorrow. Or better yet, send her a text and beg forgiveness." Ry reached for his seatbelt and had it pulled across his chest, ready to click it into place, when Whiskey growled and nudged his hand.

"You think I should go inside?"

"Woof."

Ry shook his head. Was he really going to listen to his dog? What's the worst that could happen? She could tell him to screw off. Not that he'd blame her if she did, and it might be for the best. He had a 'no relationship' policy for a reason—after the train wreck his marriage turned into, single was his best option. Or he could stop being a pussy, get out of his truck and walk into the bank and say hello. The attraction had sizzled between them at Rafe and

Meghan's wedding and hadn't abated in the weeks since he'd seen her.

"Okay, you win." Ry rubbed the dog behind his ears. "Stay. No jumping out like last time." Ry chuckled at the offended look on Whiskey's face. "You know the dog rules. No dogs in the bank. I'm sorry, but if it goes well, maybe Harmony will come out and say hi."

The large German Shepherd accompanied Ry everywhere. He was practically Ry's shadow. But there were still some places with a no-dog policy. He didn't like leaving him in the truck, but the windows were wide open, and Ry put the odds at ten to one on Whiskey in any skirmish.

The pickup's door squealed as Ry pushed it open and stretched his six-foot-two-inch frame as he stood and inhaled. He caught the perpetual scent of the Atlantic Ocean in the air. *Nothing like being home.* Yeah, he was stalling. He didn't have a clue why he had cold feet when all his non-mission time he'd fixated on her. And that was the real problem. They had one afternoon at the wedding, and he thought about her more than anyone since Cat, his ex-wife. No wonder it freaked him out.

"Stupid fucker," he mumbled as he made his way across the lot and to the bank entrance. Still, the worst that could happen was that she'd tell him to screw off. With that thought, he took another deep breath as he pulled open the glass door.

A blast of cool, stale air hit Ry as he stepped through the door and into the bank. Nodding at the guard, he looked around. In the center of the wide-open lobby area, several bank employees helped customers at desks. A few others sat in a waiting area, and three people were waiting in line for a teller, who were the only employees behind glass.

"Can I help you?" the security guard asked. His hand rested on the gun at his hip.

Ry didn't blame the man. He should have stopped at home and shaved first. It would've made a better impression on everyone. "I'm here to see Harmony Taylor."

The security guard didn't relax his stance as he passed silent judgment on Ry's appearance. The guy was obviously a rent-a-cop. They both knew that if Ry were there to cause trouble, the guard wouldn't have been able to stop him.

"Do you have an appointment? She's with a customer right now," the guard answered.

Ry followed the guard's gaze and caught his first glimpse of Harmony through the glass wall of her office.

"I'll wait for her. It's okay," Ry answered without taking his gaze off the woman he'd been fantasizing about for the past few weeks.

"You can sit over there," the guard said.

Ry glanced at him and smiled, hoping to diffuse some of the security guard's tension. "Thank you."

The guard nodded but didn't respond.

After finding a seat closest to Harmony's office, he grabbed one of the banking pamphlets from the table and thumbed through it to kill time and keep him from falling asleep. It had been a while since he had a full night's sleep, and as the adrenaline of the mission wore off, he couldn't hold back his yawns.

The longer he waited, the more he second-guessed himself. He should have sent a text or even called instead of barging into where she worked. His sister, Charli, would call him a 'bonehead' and she'd be right.

"No, that's not acceptable," a man shouted.

Ry looked up in time to see the man meeting with Harmony stand up and then lean over her desk. Instinct had Ry racing for her office without thinking. As he ran through the open doorway, he watched the man reach for Harmony. Ry grabbed him by the shoulders and pulled him away from the desk.

Harmony's violet eyes widened with surprise as she met his gaze. The man struggled to pull out of Ry's grasp, but he wasn't going anywhere. The Navy SEAL had no trouble holding on to him.

"Ry? Please let Mr. Ericson go. He won't hurt me. Will you, Harry?" She'd pushed back from her desk, but as she tried to stand, she fell and both men reached for her.

"Let me go, asshole. Or I'll press charges," Ericson growled at Ry.

"Let him go, it's okay," Harmony added as she stood successfully this time. Her cheeks flushed, making her eyes look even darker. Damn, she was even more beautiful than he'd remembered.

"If you go for her again, I'll take you out, understood?" Ry asked. Once Ericson nodded, he released him and moved closer to Harmony to stop the guy if he tried anything.

"Ms. Taylor, is everything okay in here? Do you want me to escort these gentlemen out?" The security guard asked from the doorway.

"No, Richard, I'm fine. I've got everything under control here. It was just a slight misunderstanding. Right, Harry? And my friend here is a little over-protective," Harmony answered as she raised an eyebrow at Ry.

The guard didn't look too sure he should leave, but after a moment he went back to his post at the front of the bank.

"Ry, can you give me a few more minutes? I need to finish up with Mr. Ericson."

"No need, we're done here. I trusted you. You said you

could help us, but you only fucked me out of my home. What are we supposed to do now? Barb is in the hospital, and they are saying she needs to leave. Where will we go? You took away our home." Tears ran down Ericson's cheeks even as he waved his fist at Harmony.

Ry didn't care about the man's reason. If he moved one step closer to Harmony, Ry was going to escort him out of the bank even if she didn't approve.

"Harry, I'm so very sorry. My manager even called the underwriters. We tried everything possible to stop the foreclosure. I would never have suggested you take out the mortgage if I thought you could lose your home." Harmony held out her hands in supplication. Tears pooled in her eyes.

"Don't even try, you're a lying bitch. This was probably your plan from the beginning—to take away our home. I should have known better. Banks only care about making money. But you'll be sorry. All of you."

Ry reached for Ericson, but he pulled away and stormed out of Harmony's office muttering the entire time that they'd all be sorry.

As Harmony dropped into her chair, it rolled away from the desk and tipped backward. As she squeaked in surprise, Ry pulled her up out of the chair and into his arms just before she fell ass over teacup and landed on the floor.

"Oh my God. Thank you. That's all that I'd need today, to fall on my butt in front of everyone." Tears filled Harmony's eyes as he gazed at her.

"I'm glad to be of service. Do you often have run-ins with customers like that?"

"No, not usually. Mr. Ericson is a special case..." Her voice trailed off as she stepped out of his embrace. "His wife is dying of cancer and he couldn't afford the bills.

They don't have healthcare coverage, and they didn't know what to do. Our bank has handled their accounts for years."

"And the bank is foreclosing on them?"

"Yes, it's a mess, but I can't discuss this with you. I shouldn't have said what I have already." Harmony pulled the chair closer to the desk and gingerly lowered herself into it. Then she collected the documents spread across her desk and shuffled them into a file folder.

"I didn't mean to charge in here, but from where I was sitting it looked like he was about to attack you."

"He wouldn't have. Harry and his wife have been sweethearts even though their life was falling apart. I think today was his last straw. I'm really worried about them."

"But you said it was out of your control. It's the truth, right?" Ry wasn't sure if she'd answer him since technically it was none of his business and probably against a billion and one banking rules.

"It's the truth. I don't lie, ever. Especially to customers. It doesn't fix anything though." Harmony leaned forward with her elbows on the desk and dropped her face into her hands.

Ry sat across from her in the chair Harry Ericson had vacated and searched for something to say. Anything to say to help the situation. But he was at a loss for words. And he wasn't sure how she'd feel about him touching her again. His teammates would get a kick out of it if they found out —he was the team's Don Juan—and now he didn't know what to do.

"Sometimes life just sucks, Harmony. You can't fix everything no matter how much you'd like to."

She tilted her face up and met his gaze with her tear-filled violet eyes. "I realize that. Life taught me that lesson a long time ago, but it doesn't mean I'm not frustrated and upset."

"I didn't mean that. I figured if you did all you could, then you know you tried. Sometimes that has to be enough." He should know. He'd learned that lesson the hard way.

Harmony straightened her spine and look over at him. This time, determination filled her gaze. That and something he couldn't figure out.

"I am surprised to see you, Ry. Honestly, after you didn't text or call after the second week, I figured that was it."

"I'm sorry. I planned to text you the next day. But we left on a mission the next morning. We just got back home a couple of hours ago. I changed and came straight here." Ry hoped she believed him, but he didn't know her well enough to gauge her expression.

"Is that why you look like you were auditioning for the caveman role in the next GEICO commercial?" Harmony giggled.

She giggled? Did that mean she wasn't mad at him? That she believed his excuse, even though it was right up there with the dog ate my homework. But in his life, it was what happened more than not.

"Maybe? Do you like this look?" Ry waggled his eyebrows and grinned.

"Umm. No, not really. Sorry, but I like being able to see the face hidden behind all of that hair. Did you really come straight from the base?"

"Yes, I really did. I was going to text or call, but I figured I probably pissed you off and that you'd blow me off and wouldn't answer. If I showed up, then you'd have to talk to me. Or I hoped you would. But in hindsight, I should have gone home and shaved first."

"Maybe, but it would be hard not to believe you were away when you look like this. If you showed up all bright and shiny, I might not have believed you."

"Does that mean you're not mad at me?"

"No, I'm not mad. I knew you were a Navy SEAL when we first met. I've heard from Chrissy and Meghan how often you get sent out on missions at a moment's notice. So how could I not understand?"

"There are a lot of women who wouldn't be as understanding." If he'd shown up at her office and Harmony told him to take a hike or worse, she wouldn't have been the first.

"I guess you've been dating the wrong women." Harmony grinned. The first one he'd seen since he'd gotten there.

"Probably. How about we go grab a coffee or some lunch?" When it looked like she was going to say no, Ry played his trump card. "There's someone outside who is eager to see you."

"Really? Why didn't you bring them in with you?" Harmony asked.

Ry knew the exact moment when she figured it out. Her eyes lit up, and she jumped out of her chair.

"You brought Whiskey? Oh my gosh, he must be melting in the car. Poor dog. Why didn't you say something sooner?"

"Umm, you were a little occupied when I first arrived. He's waiting in my truck. But I have the windows rolled down, and he's fine. Although definitely miffed that he couldn't come inside with me." Ry made a mental note to remember to give Whiskey an extra treat when they got home. He couldn't ask for a better wingman than the huge German shepherd.

"Let me just let my boss know I'm heading out for a

bit."

After Harmony grabbed her purse from inside her desk drawer, Ry followed her out to the lobby and waited while she ducked her head into her boss's office. He watched their interaction. All the offices looked like giant fishbowls with three of the four sides made of glass. It was probably for security reasons, by Ry would've hated being on display. He spent too much time as a ghost to work like that.

The conversation lasted longer than he'd expected, but she probably had to explain what occurred with her customer. Ry still couldn't believe how the man went off on Harmony. It made his blood boil. Ericson had a right to be upset, but not to take it out on Harmony.

That Ry was the first one to come to her rescue really worried him. What if the guy had grabbed her? Or pulled a gun? He could've shot her and then taken out half the bank customers and employees before the security guard pulled his own firearm.

Irritation colored Harmony's cheeks as she left her boss's office. As she made her way across the lobby, tension radiated through her curvy figure. Not a good sign at all. But as she approached him, she smiled, and it was like standing in the sunshine.

"Okay, we can go now."

Ry caught himself before he grasped her hand and laced their fingers together. The reaction took him by surprise. Absolutely no PDAs allowed on base, and he doubted the bank would appreciate them either. What was it about this woman? Just being close to her scrambled his brains.

Wiping his sweaty palm on the leg of his jeans before pulling open the door for her, he wondered if he'd somehow reverted to puberty. If he woke up with pimples tomorrow, he'd be pissed.

4

As Harmony stepped into the bright sunshine, some of the tension in her neck and shoulders eased. It wasn't fair what had happened to Harry and Barb. They shouldn't have lost everything because of his wife's cancer diagnosis. Tears welled in her eyes, and she blinked them away. Crying wouldn't help anything, but she'd be damned if she would just let it happen. There had to be some way she could help.

"Are you okay? You looked pretty upset when you were talking to your boss."

"Let's just say she and I don't see eye to eye about everything. She tells me I'm too soft and that the bank is in business to make money." Harmony squinted up at Ry, trying to read his expression in the sun.

"And you don't agree with her?" Ry asked.

"Well, yes, I understand that. But it's still not fair that they took everything from that poor couple. They've been through so much. Too much. The Ericsons have been customers for over twenty years, and this is how we treat them? Ugh. Sorry. You don't want to hear this. Compared to what you do every day, this is trivial."

"Not at all. I think it's horrible too, but what other options are there? I'm sure you've investigated every avenue available. Right?"

Harmony nodded. Of course, and she had found no way to stop the upcoming foreclosure. Unless she could raise a hundred thousand dollars by next week. And the odds of that happening were about a million to one. She'd spent her savings hightailing it out of Iowa and it would take her a while to build that up again. Not that she'd ever had anywhere near that kind of money.

"Yes, you're right. But it doesn't make me feel any better," Harmony murmured.

"No, but maybe this will."

They'd arrived at Ry's old truck and he'd opened the door, letting Whiskey loose. For a moment, she thought that he'd knock her over in his excitement, but he stopped right in front of her, his long tongue hanging out of his mouth as he panted. It was the closest thing to a smile that she could imagine.

Bending over, she wrapped her arms around his neck and hugged him. Holding the fluffy pooch did wonders for her mood and when she released him, her smile was genuine and not forced for the first time since Harry showed up earlier.

Harmony met Ry's gaze over the top of Whiskey's head and her heart flipped over in her chest at the desire she saw there. As she stood up and patted the dog's head, she sucked in a breath and inhaled too quickly. She started choking. *Way to go, Harmony.*

Ry patted her on the back as tears slid down her cheeks. Totally mortified, she would have run if not for Ry's hand rubbing up and down her back.

"Are you okay?" Concern wrinkled his forehead as he bent his head toward her.

"Yes," she answered when she stopped coughing. "I don't know what happened. Knowing me I probably inhaled a bug."

Ry laughed, his eyes crinkling at the corners, and tipped his head back. It was great that he was laughing, but she wanted the parking lot to open and suck her in. Whiskey rubbed against her side and put his head on her hand, nudging it until she scratched his ears. She never met a dog so empathetic. *Maybe I could steal him from Ry when he wasn't looking*? Probably not. The government might have something to say if she absconded with one of their highly trained soldiers.

"I'm sorry. I didn't mean to laugh, but you're just so damn adorable," Ry said.

"I am?" *Is he out of his mind? How is inhaling a bug and coughing up a lung adorable*?

"Yes, you are. I love that you're so real."

Harmony quirked an eyebrow as she tried to figure out if he was serious or just making fun of her. "Real? I'm not sure what you mean?"

"Most of the women I've met, except for the women dating the Black Eagle team, are always trying to be perfect. Fake, I guess. I love all the little quirky things about you."

"You mean my impersonation of Calamity Jane? Trust me, it'll get old." It obviously had for Jim when he'd run off with his secretary. Besides, her father had reminded her every day for as long as she could remember, that she was worthless.

"No, I don't think that at all." Ry slid his finger under her chin and turned her to face him. The expression in his hazel eyes took her breath away.

"Maybe I should just go back to work," she murmured, barely able to get the words out of her mouth. For a moment, she thought he would kiss her and time stood still, but then Whiskey woofed and broke the spell.

"C'mon, you need a break after what happened. Let me take you for coffee at least," Ry pleaded.

Her brain said to turn around and head back to work, but her heart did that little flippy thing and was all in for coffee, lunch, or whatever he was offering. God help her.

"Okay, but just coffee. I need to get back soon."

"I passed a Starbucks down the block. Will that work?"

"Perfect. I spend most of my lunch hours sitting outside reading. And Whiskey can come."

"Yes, he can. Do you want to drive over?" Ry looked down at her heels.

She didn't need to be a mind reader to know what he was thinking. But she'd already almost fallen twice and inhaled a bug. Surely, she could stay on her feet for a block. The universe couldn't be that cruel.

"I'll be fine. Whiskey will make sure I don't fall. Right, buddy?"

"I'm wondering if I need to be jealous of my dog." Ry grinned.

"Maybe?" Harmony winked and took Whiskey's leash after Ry attached it to the dog's collar.

They made it to the coffee shop without incident, and Harmony breathed a sigh of relief as she sat at one of the round white metal tables with Whiskey while Ry went inside to buy their coffees.

It wasn't long before Ry pushed open the door with his shoulder while balancing their drinks and a pup cup. Two women were sitting at one of the other tables and Harmony watched them ogle Ry like he was their next meal, even though he looked more like a caveman than a

Navy SEAL. As he headed over to her, she didn't try to hide her smile at their surprise.

"One iced cold brew with a pump of classic for Harmony and one Puppaccino for Whiskey." Ry placed her cup in front of her and the cup of whipped cream on the ground in front of the dog.

Then he pulled a paper bag out of his back pocket before he pulled a chair close to her side with his back against the building.

"What's in the bag?"

Ry tore open the bag to reveal two huge chocolate chip cookies. "You can't have a coffee break without a treat."

Harmony giggled. "Sure you can. I do it all the time."

"That's because you don't take your breaks with me. Cookies are the minimum, but doughnuts would be better."

She pushed down on the lid of her cup, then took a drink and saw Ry watching her. She shrugged her shoulders. She'd learned the hard way to verify it was secure. "Just making sure it's on tight."

"Got it." Then he double-checked the lid on his coffee before taking a drink.

"What did you get?"

"Just black coffee. After the last month, this is like manna from heaven."

"It's that bad?"

There was a tug on the leash and Harmony looked down to see Whiskey had stretched out under the table between her and Ry.

"Bad coffee?" He chuckled. "More like horrific. But it's better than none. That happens sometimes, too. Though not this time."

"Did everyone make it back okay?"

"Yes, the mission went well. But that's about all I can tell you. Pretty much everything we do is classified."

"Chrissy told me. She also said she gets more information because sometimes she's involved in the missions, but that Ryan hates it."

"Yup, that's true. Though now that they're engaged, most of the time she doesn't go out with them. She's come with us a few times. I don't blame Ryan. I wouldn't want my woman in danger."

"But it's her job. Isn't it?"

"Yes, it is. Ryan understands that, but it doesn't mean he has to like it. We're all a bit neanderthal when it comes to the people we care about. I think it goes with the territory. We've seen too much death and destruction."

Harmony nodded. She'd seen enough watching the evening news. "Is that why you don't date usually?" The question popped out of her mouth before she could stop it. During the last girls' night with Chrissy, Meghan, Miranda, Sky, and Dawn, she'd learned a lot about all the SEALs on the Black Eagle and Red Falcon teams. Give women pizzas, ice cream, and a lot of wine and there are no more secrets, unless they're classified. She'd even shared what happened with Jim the asshat.

"I get it. I wouldn't want anyone I loved to be in danger. But it can't always be helped."

"Exactly. But lots of women and men can't deal with it and that's why so many relationships break up. It takes a special person to be involved with a special operator or anyone on active duty."

Harmony nodded and picked up her coffee. Swirling it to mix the milk, she splashed it all over her hand and wrist. She shook her head as the heat rose in her cheeks. Could she embarrass herself any more in front of this man? It was looking unlikely. Maybe she should just knock his hot coffee into his lap and drive him away before she fell for him.

Ry grabbed a couple of napkins. He took the coffee cup from her and put it on the table, then wiped off her hand. Harmony couldn't remember the last time that someone had cared enough to do that.

"Thank you. But I could have gotten it."

"I know. I wanted to help. It gave me an excuse to touch you. But is there something you're not telling me? Are you seeing someone else?"

"No, not at all. There's no one in my life right now. I haven't had the best experience with men. I guess I'm trying to figure out why you're really here."

"Huh? You mean here with you?"

Harmony nodded and met his gaze. The intensity reflected in his eyes forced her to look away. It sounded stupid when he said it, but she couldn't wrap her brain around why he'd want to be with her.

"Well, maybe the better question would be why wouldn't I want to be with you? You're beautiful and I've never seen eyes the color of violets before. But more than that, you're funny and adorable, and interesting. You don't try to be someone you're not."

"But you're walking man-candy," Harmony said.

"What does that have to do with anything? All I know is that since we met at the wedding, I can't stop thinking about you. If you don't believe me, ask any of my team. Too bad Whiskey can't talk, he'd tell you too."

Hearing his name, the dog woofed and his tail slapped the concrete.

"But if you're not interested, all you have to do is tell me and I'll walk you back to the bank and you never have to see me again."

Was she interested in him? *Heck yeah.* But it scared her,

too. Especially after what she'd gone through with her ex. Ry waited as he held her hand. "I'm interested. Definitely. But maybe when we go out again, you should wear body armor."

He chuckled and lifted her hand to his lips and kissed it. "I'll take that under advisement, my lady. I should probably get you back to work before your boss sends a search party."

A moment later, Harmony's phone buzzed with a text message. Her boss. She didn't need to read it to know Wendy was why she wasn't in her office.

"Yup, it's like she heard us mention her." Harmony smirked. "Thank you for the coffee and the company."

"I'll walk you back. This way, we get a few more minutes with you, right Whiskey? And here, take these for later." Ry wrapped up the cookies and handed them to her. "Since you probably won't get out for lunch, at least you'll have something to snack on."

"Are you sure you don't want to bring them home with you?" Harmony asked as they headed back toward the bank.

"Nope. I need to stop at the store, anyway. Everything I left in the fridge is probably bad and will need to go in the trash."

"If you insist. It'll be a hardship to eat these, but I wouldn't want them to go to waste."

Ry chuckled. "Thank you for taking them off my hands."

They'd chatted the entire way back and Harmony hadn't tripped once. It was a minor miracle.

"I'll call you later, okay?" Ry asked. He put his hand on her arm and they stopped outside the bank.

"Yes, okay. That would be great," Harmony replied,

and then she knelt and hugged Whiskey. Ry took her hand and helped her up and pulled her into his arms.

"Is it okay if I kiss you? I've been dreaming of this for the last month."

"Yes," Harmony answered, her voice barely above a whisper.

Ry tilted her chin up and her breath caught in her throat as he lowered his lips to hers. The kiss was gentle, but it still curled her toes and filled her with need. Then it was over. He stepped back, making sure she was steady before letting go of her arms. His dazzling smile and the twinkle in his eyes sent shivers of desire racing over her skin. She didn't want it to end and barely stopped herself from reaching for him.

"I hope the rest of your day goes better than this morning did," Ry said, and took Whiskey's leash from her.

With one last pat for the fluffy dog, she went through the door Ry held for her.

Harmony stopped by Wendy's office to see if she needed anything. She'd ignored the text other than checking to see who it was from. It's not how she usually reacted at work, but what Barb and Harry were going through upset her. Couple that with her guilt that she'd caused it, and it made her want to vomit. Frustrated that her boss took the bank's side, she shouldn't have been surprised since the woman had worked there her entire career. *Doesn't anyone have empathy for others anymore?*

It irritated the crap out of Harmony, and she wished she could take the afternoon off and spend it with Ry and Whiskey, but she headed back to her desk to get some work done. Although not the work she should have been doing.

Harmony spent the afternoon researching options for the Ericsons. The foreclosure paperwork was already in progress, but from what she read about Virginia law, they should still be able to fight it.

In between helping customers, Harmony spent hours on the internet poring through pages of real estate law and still found nothing to help the couple. Her stomach churned shoulders were tight with frustration and a jabbing pain in her eye meant a full-blown headache wasn't far behind.

As she leaned back in her chair and stretched, she saw that it was already after five. No wonder she felt like crap, since the chocolate chip cookies Ry gave her were all she'd eaten. The day had been long and exasperating, except for her impromptu coffee date with Ry. Just thinking about it made her smile and eased a little of the pain in her head.

Holding on to that happy thought, Harmony straightened up her desk, locked the customer files in the drawer, and then grabbed her purse. Deciding to grab something for dinner on the way home, she headed out to the employee parking lot.

As she unlocked the door of her blue Chevy Malibu, she noticed something on her windshield. A piece of paper was tucked under one of the wiper blades. Grabbing it, she climbed into the car and locked the doors before she read it.

Hi Harmony,

Whiskey and I enjoyed our coffee date, and we hope to do it again soon. I'll call you later.

Ry

xo

. . .

After reading it twice, she tucked it into her purse with a smile on her face. Maybe it hadn't been such a bad day after all. Turning on the radio to an eighties pop station, Bonnie Tyler's voice belted out one of her favorite songs, *Holding Out for a Hero.* Harmony grinned as butterflies filled her stomach in anticipation of talking to Ry again. Maybe she'd finally found her hero.

5

After leaving Harmony at the bank, Ry ran through his list of errands. It was the same after every mission. The post office was his first stop. Then he went to the grocery store. He hadn't been kidding when he said he had nothing to eat at home. After he'd made it onto the teams, he never knew if they'd be away for a few days or a few months. He was okay with that. It's what he'd signed up for when he chose to be a SEAL. But it meant frequent trips to buy fruit, vegetables, and the fresh dog food he fed Whiskey, or he'd return to find it all rotten in the fridge.

After grabbing what he needed from the store and adding a case of beer and some snacks in case any of his teammates dropped in, he headed home for the first time since he'd left about a month earlier. He wasn't looking forward to the stuffy, closed-up smell that would welcome him. Even with the a/c on, after spending so much time either in the jungle or the desert, it took at least a day for him to acclimate. Just thinking about it made his hands damp and his pulse race. It was like reverse PTSD. *Who had that shit?*

It was the reason he rented an apartment. The last thing he needed was to return from a mission to an overgrown yard. His father would skin him alive. He'd learned that the hard way. A pang of loneliness squeezed his heart even as chuckled at the memory.

The look on his dad's face had been priceless. Ry had gone inside to say he'd finished the yard. His dad had followed him back outside to see his handiwork. Ry had deliberately skipped a section on the side of the large home. When his father saw it, his eyes nearly bugged out of his head, and he turned to Ry to read him the riot act until he saw the huge grin on his son's face. Then his mom and Charli had joined them, and they all had a good laugh at his dad's expense.

There were so many great memories of his childhood, and when he told his family he was going to enlist in the Navy, they'd supported him one hundred percent. Yeah, Ry needed to call them. It had been too long since he'd spoken to them or visited.

The B&B in the Catskills had been in their family for two generations. If he visited now, he'd end being "Ry the Repairman," or his mother would recruit him to be their tour guide. Not that he minded. There were still times he felt guilty about leaving when he heard the tiredness in his dad's voice on the phone. But his sister, Charli, loved the B&B and started promoting it on social media and now there was a waiting list to stay there. 'No room at the inn' was a real thing for the first time in years.

"C'mon boy, we're home. Finally, right?"

Ry opened the passenger door and Whiskey jumped out and sat near Ry's feet as he grabbed the groceries from the truck bed. He loved the Big Tomato, as he called it. It was perfect for the two of them, but if he and Harmony became a thing, he might need to think about upgrading his ride.

"Home sweet home. Or something," Ry said to the dog as he opened the door and let Whiskey run inside. Instantly hit with a blast of stale air, Ry sighed as he headed into the kitchen, while Whiskey searched the apartment for intruders. He could do it faster than any man and it gave him a chance to put away the groceries and fill up Whiskey's water and food bowls without the dog getting in his way.

Moving through his house, he opened the windows and the sliding glass door in the living room. The fresh air eased the knot in his shoulders and his pulse rate returned to normal. Home didn't have the same meaning anymore. Not since he and Cat broke up and there was no one waiting for him to walk through the door. Just an empty box. Not that he'd tried to change it over the last few years. It was easier to just have love 'em and leave 'em encounters than risk his heart again.

Maybe it was time to take a week off and head home, get his head back on straight. He could invite Harmony. Mom would be ecstatic. She never stopped worrying about him. But they'd just met, and she'd probably freak out at the suggestion. Did their coffee time even count as a first date? Probably not.

It was too quiet—the only sound was Whiskey's collar hitting the side of his water bowl. He grabbed a beer from the fridge and sat down in front of the TV and flipped through the channels. News, news, and more bad news. But at least it was noise.

Whiskey jumped up on the couch and rested his head on the arm. Ry grinned. The dog was something else. He watched more television than Ry. He pulled his phone out of his jeans pocket and checked for messages. He'd been hoping Harmony would send him a text, but he wasn't really surprised she hadn't. She intrigued him, and he wondered what had made her so reserved.

Was it too early to call her? Should he text her first? It was after five, but he didn't know how late the bank stayed open and he didn't want to disturb her at work twice in one day. *Fuck.* He was dithering like a boy with his first crush instead of a thirty-one-year-old with plenty of battle scars—visible and hidden.

Before he could decide whether to call or text, his phone rang. His pulsed raced, hoping it was Harmony, but was quickly replaced by disappointment when saw it was Josh, one of his teammates.

"Hey, bro, what's up?"

"I was just talking to Quinn. We're all gonna head over to the Ready Room to grab a few beers and dinner. I drew the short straw, so I got to let you know." Ry heard the smirk in Josh's voice.

"Asshat. What the fuck?"

"The way you took off to see Harmony, we didn't know if you'd be too uh busy." Josh chuckled.

"I guess I did mention her a few times over the last month."

"Ya think? You've got it bad. I hope she didn't tell you to fuck off when you showed up today."

"I got lucky. Chrissy Stillwell bailed me out on that one. They had a girls' night and explained we were out of the country."

"Did you hire her to be your personal matchmaker or what? First, she finds you the woman, then she makes sure the woman doesn't take your head off when you disappear for a month."

"Right? I guess I'll owe her a drink or six when I see her again."

"Probably. Just make sure Ryan knows why you're getting his woman drunk or you might need a medic."

"Ain't that the truth." Ry figured he'd be safe from the other SEAL, but Chrissy was lethal all by herself. She'd rescued her fiancé when they went undercover to uncover biological weapons smugglers.

"We're meeting up in about a half-hour. You coming? Or do you have a hot and heavy date?" Josh asked.

"I'll be there. Beats sitting at home by myself." Ry wanted to take back the words as soon as they'd left his mouth. The last thing he wanted to do was sound weak.

"Yeah, after spending the last month up each other's asses, it's quiet at home," Josh responded.

His words took Ry by surprise. Maybe it wasn't just him who didn't like coming home to an empty place. He was luckier than the others too, because he had Whiskey.

"Yeah. That's it, I'm missing the smell of BO and farts. Ain't nothing like it," Ry teased.

"Fuck you. Now get your smelly ass to the Ready Room so we can sniff each other. Oh, Quinn said to tell you that the first round is on you."

"Whatever. Fine. I'll see you soon."

Quinn Gallagher was their team boss, also known as Falcon One when they were on a mission. He could be a hardass and had a temper to go with his Irish ancestry, but Ry wouldn't want to serve with anyone else. Their team, like all the teams, was a well-oiled machine, even when they aggravated the fuck out of each other.

Ry decided to shower first and then call Harmony. He left Whiskey on the couch watching Animal Planet on the TV, and he grabbed his beer as he headed to the bathroom. The beard was itchy as hell and the caveman look wasn't for him.

After a steamy shower, he wiped down the mirror and

shaved. It was crazy how furry he'd gotten in a month. He needed a haircut, but that would have to wait for another day. At least when he saw Harmony, he'd look human and not like Bigfoot. If he was lucky, he'd convince her to join them at the Ready Room.

Whiskey was still on the couch, watching the television, when Ry came into the living room and grabbed his phone off the coffee table. He pulled up her contact information and clicked on her number. Anticipation had him pacing as he waited to hear her sexy voice.

Harmony kicked off her heels as soon as she stepped into her apartment. Her feet were throbbing. It was the first time she'd worn those shoes, and it would be the last time she wore them for work. Padding barefoot into the kitchen, she poured herself a glass of water and contemplated what to have for dinner as her stomach growled.

There was leftover spaghetti and meatballs from the weekend, but she'd already eaten it twice and was over it. That left eggs or her go-to dinner—a peanut butter and jelly sandwich.

"PB&J it is," she said to herself as she pulled the jar of grape jelly out of the fridge. She'd just grabbed the peanut butter when her phone rang. The sound startled her and the jar fell out of her hand onto her already sore foot. Thank goodness it was plastic, or she'd probably have ended up in the ER.

Flustered, she pulled the phone from her pocket and answered without checking the caller. "Hello?"

"Harmony? It's Ry, is everything okay?"

"Hi. Yup, everything is fine. Just me being me."

Ry chuckled. The deep rumble made her toes curl against the cool tile floor and heat pool in her belly. "Oh, okay. Do I want to know?"

"Probably not. But it's nothing serious. Just a minor mishap with the peanut butter," she answered, as she looked at the bruise forming on the top of her foot. "Before I forget, thank you for the note you left on my windshield. It was a wonderful surprise."

"I'm glad. I really had a good time and so did Whiskey. He can't wait to do it again."

"Oh yeah? Did he tell you that?" Harmony giggled.

"Yup, he'll tell you himself if you ask. Hold on, I'll put you on speaker. He's sitting on the couch watching TV with me."

"Wait, what? Dogs watch television?"

"I don't know about all dogs, but Whiskey does. He even has his favorite stations. Okay, he can hear you. Go ahead and ask him."

It should have felt silly to talk to a dog, but Whiskey seemed more human than animal. "Hi, Whiskey. Did you have a good time today?"

"Woof woof."

"Do you want to go again?" She asked.

"Woooffffff."

"See, I told you. He knows what you're saying. He's smarter than your average dog."

"I figured that out when he saved me and the wedding cake at Rafe and Meghan's wedding. He was a hero that day."

"Woof woof."

Harmony grinned, even though neither of the males on the other end of the phone could see her. "I had a good time, too. Even though what happened with Mr. Ericson was upsetting."

"Did he contact you again?"

"No, not yet. He probably won't after what happened today. I spent most of the afternoon trying to figure out a way to help him, but couldn't come up with anything. I'm heartbroken for them."

"That's because you're a sweetheart. But it's not your fault. You need to remember that."

"It feels like my fault."

"Okay, let me ask you this. If you hadn't helped with the loan, what would have happened?"

"I'm not sure. Mrs. Ericson probably wouldn't have gotten any of the treatments she needed."

"Right. I'm sure they are both thankful for the extra time they have. You helped them get that."

Harmony hadn't thought about it that way, and that was good, but they were losing everything else. The house, the business. What were they going to do?

"You're right, but now what do they do? Anyway, I know you didn't call to talk about this. How was the rest of your day?"

"Whiskey and I ran errands and just got home a little while ago. The guys called to see if I wanted to meet them at the Ready Room."

"Cool, are you going to go?" Harmony missed having a group of friends. The women she'd met through Chrissy were great, but they were all in relationships, and she only saw them when the guys were on a mission.

"I think so. Would you like to come too? We can get dinner there. Unless you've already eaten."

"But this is your post-mission unwind time, isn't it? Chrissy and Meghan said their guys do it every time." The last thing Harmony wanted to do was screw up their time. She wanted them to like her.

"Didn't Chrissy tell you that the women all come, too? Because they do."

"Yeah, but they're all in relationships. Unless something changed, you were all sitting together without women at the wedding."

"You're correct, but they all like you. It will be fine, I promise. And you'll get to see Whiskey too. Jan allows our K-9s in the Ready Room. She even added a special menu for them after they reopened."

"That's so cool. But I don't know. I have work tomorrow…" She wanted to see Ry and liked his teammates, but she really didn't want to be an interloper. All she needed was to be the Yoko Ono of the Red Falcon team. Were they even a couple yet? It seemed like they were heading there, but she wasn't sure if she was ready for that either, although she couldn't deny her attraction to Ry.

"Just say yes and give me your address, and I'll be right over. I promise I won't keep you out too late. All you have to do is tell me and I'll take you home."

"I can drive over myself," she answered, realizing that she'd just agreed to go.

"No way. This is our first date, sort of, kind of, even if we're not alone for dinner. My mother would beat me with her broom if I let you drive yourself."

"Well, then I guess you can pick me up." Harmony gave him her address.

"Great, I'll be there in about fifteen minutes. See you soon."

"See you."

Harmony put the jelly back in the fridge. No PB&J tonight. But now she had to figure out what to wear. *A date. Holy shit.* It had been a while since she'd had a real one unless you counted earlier when they had coffee.

Ry was coming to her house. *Oh. My. God.* And then

he'd bring her home later. Would he expect to come in? Chrissy had warned her about dating any of the guys she'd met at the Ready Room. Most of them were one and done. Ry didn't seem that way to her, but it didn't mean he wouldn't expect to have sex.

Did she want to have sex? The dampness in her panties said one thing, but her brain said it was way too soon. She'd only ever been with Jim and after that fiasco, was she ready to try again?

She'd drive herself crazy if she didn't stop worrying about everything. What she needed to do was get dressed and quickly before Ry and Whiskey got there. Heading into her room, she stripped out of her work outfit and stood in front of the closet. There weren't a lot of options and she decided on her favorite pair of jeans and a lavender T-shirt.

When they had coffee, Ry said how he loved the color of her eyes, so she might as well do what she could to highlight them. Then she remembered the new magnetic eyelashes she bought after seeing them all over social media. The package came last week, but she hadn't tried them yet. It seemed like the perfect time to try them, or not, depending on how they looked.

Ry would be there soon. If they were as easy to apply as all the ads said, it should be easy. First, she touched up her blush and powder. The dark circles under her eyes needed something, but she wasn't good enough at concealer to make it look natural.

Quickly skimming through the application instructions, it didn't look too bad. Then she rolled her eyes. This was her. Disaster Lass. Nothing ever went as expected. There were a few styles in the package, and she went for the ones that looked the most natural. Following the instructions, she added the magnet eyeliner.

Except she had to do it three times before she got it along her lash line. Maybe this wasn't such a good idea after all.

Shit. I need to hurry. He'd be there any minute. Her hands shook as she tried to add the lash. It was supposed to attach to her lid, except it wasn't working. Harmony pushed it onto the eyeliner, it slipped and hung off the edge of her eye like a furry black caterpillar. *Holy cow. They said this was easy. In whose world?*

The second try was worse. The lash adhered to the inner part of her eyelid, but not the rest of the liner. When she blinked, it flapped around like a wing. This was beyond ridiculous. With each attempt, Harmony grew more frustrated. A sheen of perspiration dampened her forehead. *Just great.* Even her hands were shaking as she grabbed the powder compact to fix the damage.

Harmony should have known better than to do this before a date. And not just any date—the first one in over a year. After a brief prayer to the anti-calamity gods, she took a deep breath to calm her nerves. If this didn't work, she'd give up and Ry would have to take her as she was. She wasn't a vain person, but she wanted to look her best for him and herself. Knowing she looked good always boosted her self-confidence.

Using the tip of her finger, she touched the magnetic eyeliner to make sure it was still tacky enough to work, then picked up the first lash. Well hell, it was sticky all right. The freaking thing wouldn't let go of her finger. *Sweet Baby Jesus.* She was so over this. Done. Finished. she decided she'd give it one more shot.

Too bad the damn thing didn't stick to her eye like it did to her finger. She was afraid to pull on it too hard. She didn't want to tear it. Instead, she shook her hand, trying to get it to come loose. Then it came loose and flew across the room and stuck on her lampshade. Harmony burst out laughing.

Before she could grab it, the doorbell rang. Ry and Whiskey had arrived, and she was lash-less. Err, extra-lash-less? Was that a thing? *Ugh.* She looked decent, and the T-shirt really brought out the violet in her eyes. Plastering a smile on her face, she grabbed her purse off the bed. Then she headed to answer the door and greet her dates for the evening.

6

Ry checked out Harmony's apartment complex as he waited for Harmony to answer the door. When she'd given him her address, the first thing he'd done was look it up in his map program. Relieved it was in a good part of town, he was even happier when he realized it wasn't far from his condo complex.

Getting antsy that she hadn't come to the door, he rang the bell for the second time. Had she changed her mind? She would've let him know, right? If any of his teammates could hear his thoughts, they'd laugh their asses off. Josh would be the worst, too. Calling him a crazy motherfucker as usual. *Seriously.*

When the door still didn't open, he looked down at Whiskey. The dog waited patiently at his side. Ry rubbed his ears, comforting himself more than the dog. A moment later, he sat straighter and let out a low woof as Harmony opened the door.

Ry sucked in his breath as she stood at the threshold, her gaze meeting his and then quickly dropping toward Whiskey. It was the first time he'd seen her in jeans. And holy fuck. Barely stopping himself from a wolf whistle, he gave her his best smile instead.

"You look amazing." Ry had the sudden urge to pull her against him and kiss her until neither of them could breathe. But he stopped himself. This was their first date and only the beginning of it. But holy fuck. Harmony's curvy figure was made for casual.

When they'd first met at Rafe and Meghan's wedding, she'd been all decked out, and then at the bank, she'd been wearing a suit. But seeing Harmony in jeans and a T-shirt was perfection, though he doubted she'd see it that way.

Harmony Taylor was adorable, and beautiful, with her violet eyes sparkling and her cheeks rosy with embarrassment.

"Thank you, you're not half bad yourself. It's great to see you looking like the Ry I know and…" Her voice trailed off as her cheeks filled with color. She bent down to greet his dog, and her wavy blonde hair fell over her face, covering her heated cheeks like a veil.

Could she be any more adorable?

"What? You didn't like my troglodyte look?" Ry teased.

"Umm, honestly, no, not really. But I mean—" she tripped over the words, "if you prefer the beard, it's not up to me."

"Harmony, I'm teasing, sweetheart. If you said you liked it, I'd know you were just being nice, and I wouldn't believe you."

"But, I—"

"I went home after returning from a long deployment and hadn't shaved first. My mother wouldn't even hug me until I shaved."

"Really?" Harmony giggled, and Ry's heart skipped a beat.

"SEAL's honor." Ry winked. "Are you ready to go?"

"Yes, let me just grab my purse. Do you want to come in?"

"It's probably better if I don't. We might not get to dinner." Ry couldn't help himself. He loved teasing her and seeing her blush. Seeing the different shades of pink blossom on her cheeks was like watching a sunset back home.

"Now you're just being silly." Harmony shook her head and grinned. "Your partner is terrible. But you know that already, don't you?" she said to the dog.

Damned if the dog didn't woof in acknowledgment.

"Traitor," Ry whispered to the dog as Harmony disappeared inside to get her purse.

A few moments later, Harmony was back, and Ry's breath caught as his gaze slid over her.

"Thank you for agreeing to come out with me tonight," Ry said as he placed his hand on the small of her back like he'd been doing this forever. Whiskey moved to Harmony's other side, keeping both sides of his woman safe. The thought popped into his head out of nowhere and took him by surprise, but it didn't freak him out. He'd have to analyze that later.

"I should thank you for inviting me. Isn't it a guy thing to hang out after the mission?"

"It used to be. But as so many of our friends have settled down, it's more of a welcome home celebration and an excuse for us to get together. I'm not sure who will show up, but I'd bet a couple of the Black Eagle guys will be there with their women."

"Oh, I hope so. That would be great. It feels like forever since I've seen them. Everyone has been so busy." Harmony sounded melancholy, and Ry wondered if she'd made many friends since moving to Virginia. From the hints Chrissy had dropped, he knew there was more to her move than she let on. But he would wait for her to tell him.

They'd reached his old truck, and he opened the door for her. He'd half expected her to comment on the old vehicle, but she just climbed in and buckled up. Whiskey beat him around to the driver's side, jumped in, and got comfy next to Harmony as soon as Ry opened the door.

"Have you been to the Ready Room yet?" Ry asked, as he climbed in and started the old truck.

"No, not yet. I've heard the girls talk about it. They said the food is awesome."

"It's mostly standard bar food, but Tony, the chef, talked Pam into letting him make a weekly special. It's always amazing. No one knew he was a chef at a fancy restaurant in DC."

"Really? Sky told me her mom owned the bar, but I didn't know about the rest."

"About a year ago, trouble followed Sky here from where she was living in New York. It's her story to tell, but let's just say that shit hit the fan and the Black Eagle team handled it. After that, Pam closed the bar and had it completely renovated. When it reopened last fall, the transformation was amazing. If the outside of the building hadn't stayed the same, we would've thought we were in the wrong place."

One of his favorite memories from the grand reopening party was when Murph served beer in a pink tutu. Had that taught him to stop making bets? Not a fuckin' chance in hell. He was as bad as ever, but now they didn't involve beautiful women.

Harmony's soft voice pulled him out of his reverie.

"I'm sure they needed to replace the terrible memories," Harmony said thoughtfully.

Ry nodded. It had been the reason for the reno, but it

surprised him that Harmony picked up on it. Again, he wondered what had driven her away from her home.

"We're here." Ry pulled into the parking lot of the strip mall home of the Ready Room. It still looked like a dive bar from the outside, and it kept the tourists away, which was fine with him and the rest of the SEAL teams that made it their hangout.

"That's it?" Harmony seemed surprised.

Ry grinned. "Yup. Don't worry. I wouldn't take you to a dive."

Whiskey woofed and nuzzled her arm.

"Don't worry, big guy. I'm not gonna chicken out," she said, and rubbed the dog behind his ears.

Ry shook his head as he got out of the truck. Sheer craziness. He was jealous of his dog. Fucking pitiful. Knowing Whiskey's intuition, he knew it, too. *What the fuck?*

It's like she put a spell on him. Not that he believed in magic, but how else could he explain it? He'd sworn off relationships after his cheating ex broke his heart. But somehow Harmony had stitched it back together, and he'd be damned if he knew how it happened. Oh yeah, he was in big trouble. And as soon as he walked Harmony into the bar, his teammates would know it, too. Although Josh probably realized it before Ry. They'd been closer than brothers since BUD/S and knew each other better than they knew themselves.

After Harmony climbed out of Ry's truck, Whiskey jumped down and stood next to her in the crowded parking lot of the strip mall. Not what she'd expected at all when he told her they were going to the Ready Room. She'd figured it was in one of those buildings with the flashing neon lights outside advertising the many beers on tap. She may never have been inside a bar, but she'd driven past more than her fair share.

"Is Whiskey allowed inside?"

"Yes, Pam allows all of us to bring them. She even has a special menu for them," Ry replied as attached the dog's leash.

"That's very cool. This is definitely a first for me."

"Being in a bar that allows dogs?" Ry asked as they made their way across the parking lot and toward the front door.

"Yes, but um, I've never actually been inside a bar." Harmony's stomach flip-flopped at her admission. It was times like this she felt like such a hick. She was, but still, sometimes it sucked to have led such a sheltered life. But her father would have killed her if he ever heard she'd stepped inside a bar.

"Really? I like that I'm going to take you to your first one."

She'd expected him to be surprised, but not thrilled about it. "Yup, my first bar."

"You're going to love the Ready Room. Sure it's a bar, but with all that Pam and Tony did to the place, it's a really great place to hang out."

"I trust you." Harmony nodded.

Ry winked at her, then pulled open the wooden door. She took a deep breath to settle the butterflies running rampant in her tummy. She did trust Ry, even though it was much too soon in their whatever this was between them. So the sudden attack of nerves didn't make sense. Just plain old silly. It was just a building with music, alcohol, and food. Absolutely no reason for her to not go inside. Even if she could hear her father's angry voice resounding in her head. So real. She shuddered, and goosebumps rose on her arms.

Ry must have felt the change in her. He gave her a questioning look and squeezed her hand in encouragement. Whiskey rubbed against her free hand and nudged her with his nose. And just like that, her butterflies settled. Surrounded by her fierce protectors, she was safe. Her heart knew it even if her head couldn't quite catch up as she accompanied them inside.

The aroma of French fries and burgers wafted over Harmony, and her stomach growled in response. Not that she had to worry about anyone hearing it over the loud music.

Ry waved at an older woman as they passed the massive bar and headed toward the back of the large table-filled room. They stopped a few times for Ry to chat with people he knew, and each time he introduced her as his girlfriend.

Girlfriend?

Seriously?

This was their first official date, and they were going to be with a bunch of friends. Did that really count? Just being with Ry was happiness in a can, but she wasn't sure about the rest. Attraction sizzled between them from the first moment they'd met, but maybe it was just lust. Once they'd done the deed, he'd probably be done with her.

"Got room for two more?" Ry asked.

Harmony looked up from focusing on her feet. She'd been doing all she could to keep from tripping in the crowded bar. Ry squeezed her hand in encouragement. He probably thought she was nervous, and she was, but not like she had been.

She looked up to see two tables pushed together crowded with Ry's teammates and some of the Black Eagle team and her friends. He'd been telling the truth when he'd said it was more like a huge welcome home party instead of the team blowing off steam.

"About time you got here, asshole," a dark-haired guy with broad shoulders and a smirk on his face shouted over the music.

"Fuck you, Josh," Ry responded, then turned to Harmony and smiled. "He's just an ass. Don't mind him."

Harmony smiled and nodded, then giggled. How many times had she heard, 'just smile and nod?' and now she'd done it for real. *Oh man, I'm such a dork.*

A huge red-headed SEAL stood and grabbed a couple of chairs from the neighboring table.

"We always have room." She heard the SEAL's deep voice easily over all the background noise.

"Thanks, Quinn. You remember Harmony, right?" Ry asked as they shook hands.

"Of course. How are you? We're a little wild after our last mission, but we don't bite," he said and grinned.

Dang, he was sexy, but not like Ry. As much as she'd liked them in their dress whites at the wedding, seeing them in casual clothes was the sexiest thing ever. If the mean girls back home could see her now, they'd just die.

Harmony followed Ry around the table, stopping to hug Meghan, Chrissy, and Sky as she made her way to the chairs Quinn grabbed for them.

"It's great to see you," Meghan said as she pulled her into a tight hug. "It's been too long."

"You just got back from your honeymoon. I think you've been more than a little tied up." When she realized what she'd implied, Harmony felt her cheeks heat.

It didn't seem to bother Meghan at all. She laughed and said, "Fuck yeah."

"Exactly." Harmony said, relieved she hadn't insulted

her friend. The friendship was still new with these women, and she didn't want to do anything to make them mad at her.

But they'd all been busy. Meghan on her honeymoon, Chrissy on a mission—or two, it was hard to keep track—and Dawn was always busy with her kids.

Sky hugged her next after she put two pitchers of beer on the table. "How are you, Harmony? I'm so glad you came tonight. Josh said Ry going to ask you to come with him."

Harmony looked over at Josh, who was deep in conversation with Rafe, Meghan's husband. Rafe took over the Black Eagles when they'd promoted Dawn's husband, Jake.

"I'm glad I did. Honestly, after seeing the outside, I'm totally in love with the inside." Harmony hoped she didn't sound rude and worried her bottom lip between her teeth.

"I know, right? Mom wanted to do it for years. It just took the right motivation. Remind me at next girls' night and I'll tell you the whole sordid story. Everyone else already knows. Or you could ask Ry," Sky said and tipped her head toward her date.

"He mentioned you had a complete renovation but said it wasn't his story to tell."

"That's what I love about these guys. They all have so much integrity and loyalty. You could trust them with your life even if they didn't know you. But if they fall for you, expect total alpha overload." Sky winked.

"Hey, Sky, stop scaring my date," Ry said with mock horror.

Harmony smiled, but Sky's words made the little hairs on the back of her neck stand up. After her father's cruel treatment and strict rules, alpha overload was definitely not what she wanted in a relationship.

They settled at the table, and Ry draped his arm across the back of her chair and squeezed her shoulder.

Considering what she'd just learned from Sky, she should be uncomfortable, but it was the opposite. Warmth slid along her spine and shoulders, and she leaned against him.

"What's going on in that pretty head of yours?" Ry whispered close to her ear. Then he lifted the pitcher as he raised his eyebrows.

After her nod, he filled two glasses and set one in front of her.

"Nothing really, why?"

"You look serious. Is this too much? We can leave and I'll take you somewhere quieter." Concern was obvious in his expression.

"No, it's not that. Sky made me wonder about the whole alpha thing. And you surprised me when you introduced me as your girlfriend." Even as the words left her mouth, Harmony winced inside. Why had she just blurted that out? She could have brought it up when they were alone, not in front of his teammates and friends, when they could barely hear themselves speak.

She needed to get out more with people her age who enjoyed doing things. People who didn't spend all their time working and hiding from life. Wasn't that the reason she moved to Virginia in the first place? To escape not only her father and her ex, but to have a life she could enjoy.

"Well, I'm not sure about the whole alpha thing, be we do tend to be overprotective. But if you ask Chrissy, she'll tell you how to deal with that. Ryan was probably the worst of all of us." Ry chuckled. "As for saying you're my girlfriend, I apologize if it upset you. It wasn't my intention at all. Probably more like wishful thinking. Plus, I didn't want anyone else hitting on you. Most of the women here are regulars, either in a relationship, or looking to take a SEAL to bed."

Harmony gazed around the room. That's when she saw groups of women standing by the jukebox or sitting at the bar, their gazes focused on the tables filled with men. Dang it, their expressions were positively feral.

"It's not that you upset me, exactly. Just didn't expect it." Harmony reached up and squeezed his hand where it rested on her shoulder.

"Maybe you'd rather hang out with one of them?" Ry asked with a devious twinkle in his gaze.

Harmony was on to him this time. "Hmm, I could go check them out? A couple of them are kinda cute. But then so is Quinn." She tried to say it with a straight face, but she'd barely finished speaking when she giggled.

"Funny woman. I'll get you back for that."

"I'm not worried. Whiskey will protect me. Right, buddy?"

The big German shepherd moved between them and sat down.

Ry chuckled. "You remember whose dog you are, right?"

Harmony took a drink of the beer and realized she felt more relaxed than she had since she moved to Virginia Beach. It was due to Ry and his friends, and she hadn't fallen or tipped over a beer yet.

As she listened to the friendly chatter around her, she glanced over the menu and decided on a burger and fries.

7

Ry reintroduced Harmony to all the guys at the table. She hoped that she'd remember their names this time. Although it wasn't her strength, it usually took a few times before the name stuck with the face. It embarrassed her father, and he'd called her stupid more than once. He'd called her worse too. But this was a date, her first real one with Ry, and she didn't need to be thinking about the past.

Quinn involved Ry in conversation, but she didn't mind. Surrounded by all this happiness was almost more intoxicating than the beer.

"It's great to see you again, Harmony," Fergus "Doc" O'Brien said. He was sitting on her left side.

"Thank you. I'm happy to see you, too." *Ugh, small talk.* She sucked at it, big time. The last thing she wanted to do was embarrass Ry.

Fergus must have picked up on her discomfort and smiled. "Ry said you worked in a bank?" He said it like a question.

Questions she could deal with. Collecting her thoughts, she took a sip of her beer.

"Yes, I have for a while now. I worked for the same bank back in Iowa and was able to get a transfer."

"That had to make the move a lot easier. Having to find work in a new place would be hard."

"Oh yeah. I don't think I would have had the courage to do it if I didn't have a job waiting for me here." Again, her mouth moved before her brain caught up. The sympathetic gaze in his light-blue eyes said he understood, and he didn't push her for answers.

"Can't beat that, for sure," Fergus replied, his voice deep enough that she heard him without having to lean closer.

What was it with all these guys? Did the SEAL recruitment team require more than killer skills? Maybe big, sexy, and gorgeous was also a requirement from what she'd seen already. It had to make staying hidden that much harder. Just thinking about Ry in danger made her stomach turn over and she lost her appetite.

"All I needed was to find an apartment, and there were plenty to choose from."

What she didn't say was that the best of all was when Chrissy and Meghan walked into the bank and sat down in front of her desk. It was the day she'd met her first friends, and not just in Virginia, but in all her life—or friends her dad hadn't chased away.

Fergus nodded. "Do you enjoy it? Working at the bank, I mean."

"Usually, although it's a lot different here than it was back home. I lived in a small town and mostly everyone knew each other. Virginia Beach is definitely not a small town."

Fergus chuckled. "No, that's for sure. Before I joined the Navy, I lived in a small town in Wyoming. So, I get it."

"Yes. But most people are friendly. My boss and I don't

always agree. She's all about the bank and not the people. I'm used to more flexibility and here it's all stick to the rules."

"It sounds a lot like the Navy."

"I guess it does." Harmony smiled.

"Unfortunately," Ry chimed in.

Harmony turned her head to find him watching her, and then exchange glances with Fergus. Had he asked his friend to talk to her? Sky's early remark about alphas slid through her thoughts like an ugly worm. Planting seeds of worry. Then she told herself she was being silly. Fergus was being polite to the new girl.

"I wonder how many jobs are?" Fergus asked.

"Probably most of them," Ry replied as his hand kneaded her shoulder, releasing the tension tightening her muscles.

"Weird. But you're right, we all have rules to follow. Even if you have your own business. Certain things always need to be done," Harmony mused. Owning her own business was one of her dreams. But it would probably have to be a bubble wrap store just to make sure she didn't destroy all her products.

"Yes, but not all of them hurt others when they're made," Ry said with an angry edge to his voice.

Harmony nodded and wondered if he was thinking about Harry Ericson or something he'd done on his last mission. This time, she'd wait until they were alone to ask. If it was his job, he wouldn't be able to tell her. If it was about Harry, maybe he'd be able to help her come up with a solution to help.

"Excuse me," Quinn said from Ry's other side. Then he walked away from the table with his phone to his ear.

"Well fuck, we just got back," Ry grumbled.

"They wouldn't send us out again unless they didn't

have a choice. It's probably just a call. I'd bet Rafe would get a call before us."

"I hope so."

"Am I missing something?" Harmony asked.

Fergus grinned. "Ry is worried that Quinn's call is about a new mission."

"Oh, you mean you might have to leave, already? You just got back." Harmony tried to keep the whininess out of her voice.

"Not likely," Rafe said. "Fergus is right, they'd send us out first. We didn't just return from a mission."

"Do you all have supersonic hearing or something? It's loud in here and you heard our discussion from over there?" Harmony asked.

"Yes, we're fitted with special devices."

Harmony was sure she had a look of horror on her face. Until Ry and Fergus busted out laughing.

"He's teasing you. We're just used to being tuned in all the time," Ry said, and grinned.

"Ahh, I see how you are. Tease the hayseed," Harmony tried to sound hurt but couldn't hold back her chuckle.

"I'm sorry, Harmony, but it was too easy," Rafe said, attempting to sound like he was sorry.

"You better not be fucking with my friend," Meghan said as she appeared behind Harmony. "You'll be sorry."

Ry laughed. "No tumble in the sheets for you, Rafe."

"C'mon, Spitfire. I only teased her a little," Rafe said.

Meghan winked at Harmony, and she giggled. Would that be her and Ry someday?

"Want to come to the ladies' room with me?" Meghan asked.

"Sure."

"We'll be right back," Meghan said to the SEALs and gave Rafe a quick kiss on the lips.

"Where's mine?" Ry asked.

Before Harmony could answer, Meghan responded. "Suck it, Ry."

The guys' laughter followed them as they walked away.

They'd barely entered the restroom when Meghan peppered Harmony with questions.

"Are you okay? Ry told Josh, and he told Rafe about what happened at the bank today. It sounded fucking horrible."

"Really? It spread like wildfire, huh? Yes, I'm fine. Just upset for my client." Harmony added another item to the mental list of things to discuss when they were alone.

"Well, I think he was just so shocked that it happened. He really likes you. It surprised the guys, but Chrissy and I knew you two were fucking perfect for each other."

"Whoa, there. This is our first date. Don't go picking out china patterns or anything. Besides, I bet the first time I spill a cup of coffee or beer on him, he'll run for the hills."

"No way. You don't know much about SEALs, do you?" Meghan asked.

"Only what I saw on TV when SEAL Team Six killed Osama bin Laden. And, well—"

"What?" Meghan asked, clearly curious.

"Just what I learned in the romance novels I've read. But I'm sure they make most of that up." Harmony glimpsed herself in the mirror. Her cheeks were turning pinker by the moment as heat slid up her neck and into her face. *Gawd.*

"You are so freakin' cute. Or maybe it's innocence." Meghan hugged her.

"I'm not innocent. Just cautious. My father would have killed me if he found me reading romance." Harmony moaned. When would she learn to keep her mouth shut?

"You're kidding, right?"

Harmony shrugged her shoulders and sighed. "I wish, but he's one reason I moved here. I needed to get away from him. It was pure luck I saw the posting for this job on the bank's website.

"I'm so sorry. Should we jump in the car and go take the fucker out?" Meghan's cheeks flushed with anger.

"No, definitely not. And you need to promise not to tell Rafe if he's going to tell Ry. Sky said they were overprotective guys, and I don't need to set him off. I've had more than my share of being controlled."

"Oh Har, he wouldn't ever try to control you. But it would horrify him that anyone, especially family, hurt you."

"Maybe, we'll see. But I need you to promise me, Meghan. Please."

Meghan sighed and shook her head. "I promise not to tell Rafe. But I'm not happy about it."

Harmony smiled. "I know, I can tell. But like Ry didn't tell me Sky's story, this is mine to tell if I decide he needs to know."

"I think I misjudged you a little," Meghan said, as she quirked an eyebrow.

"How so?"

"Aww Har, don't worry, it's not bad. I think you're a lot stronger than you come across or give yourself credit for. You're going to be great for Ry."

Harmony shook her head. "I think you're all a little crazy. We barely know each other."

"We'll see. I knew it almost right away when I met Rafe. There was something different about him. It was one of the worst times of my life, but I'd go through it all again if it meant I'd end up with him."

"Chrissy told me a little of what you went through with your brother and the Taliban. I couldn't believe you went to Afghanistan by yourself."

"Yeah, it was stupid, but all I could think about was helping my brother, and it was the only option I could come up with. I'd be dead if not for Rafe and the team."

"It's almost like a book," Harmony responded.

"Yes, and if I have my way, it will be. It'll be fiction, but since I have direct knowledge of a classified mission, the DOD has final approval before I can publish it. So much red tape and hoops to jump through."

"I will buy it," Harmony exclaimed.

"Thank you." Meghan smiled. "I guess we should go back before they send out a freaking search party for us."

"Are you serious?"

"Yup, it's their protector instinct. They can't help it. You just have to remember it's done with love, not malice."

Harmony wasn't sure how she felt about any kind of control, and if Ry tried to lock her down, she'd have something to say about it.

"Ry is one of the good guys. Just try to keep an open mind, okay?" Meghan asked.

"I'll try—" A knock on the ladies' room door interrupted Harmony's response.

Meghan shrugged and opened the door with a grin, revealing a worried Rafe and Ry. Then she turned and winked at Harmony, as if to say, 'see, I told you so.'

"Everything okay?" Rafe asked as his gaze traveled over Meghan.

"Yes, my love. We were chatting. What trouble could we get into in the restroom? Seriously, dude." Meghan stepped into his arms for a hug.

"You can ask me that after what happened to Sky in this building," Rafe replied.

The storm clouds on Rafe's face dissipated as he held his wife.

"Do you want to take this out of the doorway?" Ry asked as he stood just behind them in the hallway.

"Sorry, bro." Rafe kept his arm around Meghan as they stepped out of the way.

Harmony watched as Ry stopped at the threshold. She gave him brownie points for not grabbing for her or being short-tempered. All her internal alarm bells should've been ringing, but they weren't. None had rung when he'd rushed into her office at the bank, either. His presence didn't freak Harmony out at all—no strangling feeling, no dread churning in her stomach like when her father would track her down.

"Are you okay? Did Fergus upset you? Or Rafe?" Ry asked, his brow wrinkled with concern.

"I'm fine. Just regular old girl-talk. Neither of us realized we'd been chatting for so long."

"No problem. As long as you're okay. That's all that matters." This time, Ry smiled and held out his hand.

"I didn't mean to worry you," she said as she took his hand.

"Rafe grew concerned when he realized it'd been more than a half-hour since you and Meghan left. They've been through a lot…"

"Yeah, she's told me some of her story. It's unbelievable."

"It sure is. Ready to go back to the table, or would you rather leave?" Ry asked as she took his hand.

"We can stay, unless that old red truck turns into a pumpkin at nine pm." Harmony giggled.

"Hey, no denigrating my truck. It was my grandpa's

and I love that thing. It is getting harder to find parts for it, though. But as long as I can keep it running, I will."

"That's so sweet."

"Nah, probably stupid and definitely expensive. But I have so many memories of riding around in it with him. Hang around long enough, and I'll tell you some." Ry waggled his eyebrows like some dirty old man.

Harmony giggled all the way back to the table, and after she sat down, she realized she hadn't tripped even though she wasn't paying attention to where she'd been going.

After another hour passed, Harmony had trouble hiding her yawns and Ry had noticed more than once. If she'd been home, she'd have fallen asleep with one of her romance novels in her hand and her glasses on her face. Instead, she was in an actual bar, sitting with a bunch of real-life heroes, and wondering how she'd gotten so lucky.

"I love your smile. What's got you grinning in between yawns, or should I say who?" Ry whispered into her ear.

When Harmony turned her head, it put their lips within inches of each other, and her pulse pounded in her ears. All she had to do was lean forward the tiniest bit, and they'd kiss. But that would take way more courage than she possessed, even if his teammates weren't sitting with them.

"Actually, you kinda did. I was thinking about how lucky I was to be sitting here with all of you."

"Oh yeah? All of us, huh?"

"Don't be jealous. You're my favorite, but if you tell anyone, I'll deny it."

Ry threw back his head as laughter poured out. Then he pulled her into a quick hug.

"We're going to get going. Harmony has work tomorrow," Ry announced as he helped her up. Whiskey came out from under the table.

“And you have PT at five. Don’t be late,” Quinn said. Then smiled as everyone groaned.

“Fuck, Q. After the month we’ve had, can’t you push it ‘til seven?” Josh asked.

Harmony thought he was kidding about the five am PT until Josh asked for a later time. That was just crazy talk. Seven was a much more reasonable hour.

“You’re a bigger hardass than I am,” Rafe joked.

“Fuck you, Buchanan. No one is worse than you. Okay, seven it is,” Quinn said, and then added, “But that’s only for tomorrow.”

Harmony hugged Chrissy, Sky, and Meghan as she reminded her of the promise she’d made. After saying good night to all the guys, she took Ry’s hand as they made their way to the parking lot, and he helped her get into Grandpa’s red truck.

8

Ry got Harmony and Whiskey settled in the truck, then settled in behind the wheel. "Did you have a good time?"

She turned toward him and smiled. "Oh yes, it was fun. It was great to see the girls again, too."

"I'm happy to hear that. I wondered a few times if I upset you. Other than the whole girlfriend thing."

"Eh, it was a surprise to hear it. I understand why you said it, although I still think it's kind of quick. But it looks like I'm the only one who does." Harmony pushed a lock of hair behind her ear.

It was one of her tells, and Ry wondered if Meghan upset her when they went for their girl-talk. "I don't know what you mean."

"Meghan said all the guys were happy you'd found someone, and that we were the perfect couple."

"Seriously? She told you that?" It surprised Ry to hear that. It had to have been Josh wagging his dick beaters to Rafe, since he knew how attracted Ry was to Harmony. "And that makes you unhappy?"

"No, not unhappy. I really like you, but I don't know you and I already have trust issues after my ex-fiancé cheated on me and let me catch him a week before our wedding. It was horrible. My brain says to run away from you, as fast as I can. But my heart, well, that says I can trust you. And that scares me." Harmony sighed when she finished and rubbed her face against Whiskey's head.

Ry's heartstrings tugged for what she'd been through, and he understood how she felt. Hell. He had an ex-wife who'd done almost the same thing. They didn't know much about each other, but they could change that if he didn't have another mission too soon.

"I'm sorry, sweetheart. I hate that your ex treated you like that. It really sucks. I'd like to teach him a lesson, but it's his loss and my gain. And you're right, we don't know each other well, but if you're up for giving this a chance, so am I."

"I'd like to give it a chance. But I'm a lot different from all the women around here. And a super klutz. I aggravate people with my clumsiness."

"And that's what makes you wonderful. I don't want someone who is only after me to say she slept with a SEAL or to get my benefits. You're sweet, compassionate, and beautiful. You listen when people talk and you don't need to be the center of attention."

"Oh, heck no. I prefer when no one notices me."

"Why? You're smart and funny. You shouldn't hide yourself away." Ry wondered just how badly her ex-fiancé had treated her to make her want to hide from the world instead of letting her beautiful light shine.

"Until you, nothing good has ever come from being noticed," Harmony murmured.

Ry wondered if she realized how much she just admitted, but it flooded his chest with warmth. He ached to take her into his arms and comfort her. To inhale her sweet scent and kiss her until bliss colored her cheeks and swept away her sorrow. But it would have to wait a bit longer. He doubted she'd appreciate being hugged around Whiskey even if the dog would love the attention.

They'd almost reached her road when he had to pull over for a fire truck and two police cars to zoom past.

"Oh no, I hope it's not an accident, and there are no injuries," Harmony said, as she watched the vehicles drive by.

"Me, too. It's a good sign that we haven't seen an ambulance." *Or it had already arrived.*

"That's true. Unless someone called them first," Harmony mused.

There was no putting anything over on this woman. One more thing to add to his list of things he loved about Harmony. Or if not love, then a major case of the likes. He'd never felt this way before, not even with Kat.

"Yeah." There really wasn't anything else to say. Ry hoped they didn't have to pass the scene. But reality doused that wish quick enough.

As they turned the corner, they watched the emergency vehicles pull into the parking lot of Harmony's apartment complex. His protector genes kicked in and Ry's switch flipped from relaxed, easy-going guy to SEAL on alert. Especially when he saw it was a car fire.

"Oh no," Harmony exclaimed, and covered her mouth with her hand before turning toward him. "I think that's my car."

Ry pulled into the parking lot and parked as close as he could get to her building. Flames licked the sky as the firefighters extinguished the remains of the burning car carcass. If they couldn't find the VIN number, Ry didn't have a clue how they'd figure out who owned the vehicle. Even though Harmony insisted it was her Chevy Malibu.

"Stay here with Whiskey, while I see what I can find out," Ry said as he released his seatbelt and opened his door.

"No, I'm coming too. Especially if it's my car that's burned to a crisp." Harmony had already opened her door and jumped out.

"Wait. We don't know what's going on. You could be in danger. Let me find out what they know—"

"I understand you're trying to protect me, but I will be fine. We're surrounded by first responders. What could possibly happen?" she asked.

Ry didn't have an answer, except his gut instinct said she should stay in the truck. But no way would she accept that as a reason. "C'mon boy, you're coming too. Keep an eye on her, okay?" Ry instructed the canine.

"I heard that."

He'd wanted her to hear him and to know that they wouldn't let anything happen to her, even if she didn't want the protection. The situation could literally blow up at any moment, and he'd do what it took to keep her safe.

As they made their way through the gathered crowd, he took Harmony's hand and kept her close. It's not how he'd planned the evening to end, and he hoped they'd find her car safe and sound. But as they got closer, he realized she was correct as he counted the numbered spaces leading up to what remained of the incinerated vehicle. *Fuck.*

Harmony's fingers tightened as she realized her fear was true. "Nooo. How could this happen?" Her eyes grew wide with horror and filled with unshed tears.

Ry's heart squeezed in his chest, and he pulled her more tightly against his side. But he had the same question.

Cars didn't just ignite on their own. It needed help, and whoever helped this one had known what they were doing.

"You need to step back," a police officer directed.

"But that's my car. What happened?" Harmony's tear-filled voice made him want to hunt down the person who did this.

"It's your car? Are you sure?" The officer turned around and looked at the still-smoking metal frame.

"Yes, it's my apartment number on the parking spot. I need to know what happened? Was anyone hurt?"

"Hold on. I'll get someone to come talk to you. But stay here, ma'am." The cop waited until Harmony nodded in acknowledgment before he went over to a male with salt and pepper hair dressed in a wrinkled suit. All he was missing was the raincoat to resemble Detective Columbo, one of his favorite TV detectives.

"What's he doing?" Harmony asked.

"My guess is he's talking to the detective in charge of the scene. I'm sure he'll want to talk to you. If you don't want to do this alone, just tell him you want me to stay with you," Ry said. He didn't want her out of his sight. His gut said this wasn't an accident.

"They can't think I did this. What would be the reason? I need my car. How am I going to get to work? I don't have the money to replace it." Harmony's voice rose as she started to hyperventilate.

Ry wrapped his arms around her and leaned her head against his chest. He rubbed up and down her back, trying to soothe Harmony as sobs wracked her. Hot tears soaked his T-shirt, but her breathing settled. Whiskey brushed against his leg to get closer to her. As Ry watched, the dog nuzzled her hand trying to offer his brand of comfort. Whatever she needed, he wanted to be the one to give it to her.

The sensation of being observed raised the hairs on the back of Ry's neck. As he surveyed their surroundings, his gaze connected with the detective's assessing one. Then the man headed toward them.

"Sweetheart, the detective is coming. Remember, none of this is your fault. They're just trying to figure out what happened."

Harmony lifted her tear-stained face and nodded. Ry wished with all his heart that he could whisk her away and kiss her until she shivered with desire instead of shock.

While Harmony registered Ry's words, she couldn't fathom how her car, her only means of transportation, no longer existed. If it was an accident, then she should count herself lucky that it hadn't caught fire while she was driving. But the alternative, one she didn't want to consider, seemed a lot more likely. But who? She hadn't lived in Virginia long enough to bring this type of wrath down on her. Unless her father had tracked her down and this was part of his plan to get her back to Iowa and under his control.

Queasiness threatened to make her vomit all over Ry as saliva pooled in her mouth and bile rose up her throat. Gulping down air like her life depended on it, she focused on the firm muscles beneath her hands.

"Are you okay, baby? You're pale as a ghost. Do you need to sit down?" Ry questioned, his forehead wrinkled with concern.

"I'm better now," Harmony replied, and focused on taking short, measured breaths.

Ry lifted the bottom of his T-shirt and wiped the tears

from her face, then dropped a quick kiss on the tip of her nose.

It was the sweetest thing anyone had ever done for her. Snuggling against his chest, she inhaled his masculine scent and let his calm presence ease her stress.

"Ma'am, my officer said this is your car."

The police detective's gravelly voice sent her anxiety spiraling out of control. Harmony jumped out of Ry's arms, and her pulse pounded so loud she wondered if Ry could hear it.

"Yes, sir. That's my parking space, and I parked there earlier."

"Can you follow me so we can talk?" The detective lifted the caution tape for her to follow him.

Harmony held onto Ry's hand for dear life. Even if it made her a chicken, when she looked up at the detective, she saw her father's furious face.

"Sir, you can stay here."

"No. He's with me, the dog, too." Harmony didn't know where the determined voice came from, but she sighed with relief when the detective nodded.

Ry squeezed her hand and whispered, "That's my girl."

The curious glances from the onlookers made Harmony's skin crawl. What if her father was in the crowd? Watching her? Just waiting for his chance to grab her and drag her back home. When she'd moved to Virginia, she'd prayed that it was too far for him to bother tracking her down like a lost dog. But maybe she'd been wrong. Acid churned in her stomach and perspiration dampened her forehead.

Finally, the gruff detective stopped in front of a dark blue sedan.

"I'm just going to take some notes, okay?"

Harmony nodded, Ry's presence by her side the only

thing keeping her from running away. This reminded her of home so much that she expected the detective to stuff her into the back of the car and drive her home. Her father would send the sheriff after her whenever she was late.

The cop's tone was softer now when he asked his questions. "Can I have your name?"

Maybe he'd realized that he was scaring the crap out of her.

"Harmony Taylor, T, A, Y, L, O, R."

"Got it. And your address and phone number?"

"It's that unit over there." She pointed, then shook her head and rattled off the full address and the apartment number even though it was on the parking spot.

"Do you remember what time you parked your car?"

"Umm, it was a little after five pm. I came straight from work."

The detective nodded as he made notes.

Ry and Whiskey stood on either side of her like her personal protection, and she'd be forever grateful. Even if her father showed up, Ry wouldn't let him steal her away. She knew it without a doubt.

"Which bank?"

Harmony told him about the bank, including the branch number and address, then stole a glance at Ry. He smiled, encouraging her.

"Great, thank you. Do you know if the complex has cameras?"

"No, I'm sorry. I never thought to ask," Harmony replied. Should it have been something she checked for? She'd only lived at home and in their small town, no one locked their doors. Putting up cameras would have been an insult to your neighbors.

"It's okay, we'll check with the office in the morning." Then he made more notes.

Harmony was antsy as she fought the urge to run and hide.

"Are you okay? Would you like to sit in the back of the car?"

"No," Harmony exclaimed. The last thing she wanted to do was get into the police car, marked or unmarked. But she hadn't meant to shout and bring the attention back to her.

"This is very nerve-wracking for her," Ry added.

"I'm sure. You're not in trouble, young lady, unless you've done something wrong?" the detective asked.

"No, nothing. I've only lived here a few months. The car is new to me. I purchased it used in Iowa before I moved here."

"And what's your name, sir?" the cop asked Ry.

"Chief Petty Officer Ryder Purcell, stationed at JEB Little Creek-Fort Story, sir."

The detective's expression softened. "And is this your dog, Ms. Taylor?"

"No, sir, he's Ry's teammate." Harmony wasn't sure how to refer to Whiskey, so she improvised.

"That's right, he's part of our TEAM, a K9 soldier."

The cop looked down at Whiskey and he let out a low growl and moved to stand in front of Harmony as if to say back off. Sky's words came back to her. Maybe it wouldn't be so bad to have an alpha protector for a boyfriend, after all.

"Were you home all evening?"

Harmony looked up at Ry, and he squeezed her hand. "No, I was out with Ry, Ryder. We were at the Ready Room. We were with a lot of friends, so we have an alibi."

The detective chuckled. "You don't need an alibi,

you're not a suspect. I just need all of this for the police report. You'll need a copy to file a claim with your insurance company."

"Oh, right. I didn't even think about that." Harmony breathed a sigh of relief. She shouldn't be a suspect. Based on her experience with the police, her trust level was nonexistent.

"Speaking of that, do you have your insurance card and vehicle registration? We're waiting on the tow truck to take your car to the station. The crime scene techs have to wait for the vehicle to cool off before finishing their investigation."

"Oh no, they were in the glove compartment. I'll have to get copies."

"It's okay, we can get it. Just one more question. Do you know of any reason someone would do this to your car?"

"I really don't. Like I said, I've only lived here a short time and I don't think I've made any enemies." Harmony hesitated, and the detective picked up on it.

"It looks like you thought of someone…"

"Well, it's probably crazy, but maybe my father. But he should be in Iowa."

Ry's intake of air made her cringe. Now she was going to have more of her story to tell. She doubted he'd let her get away with not telling him everything.

"Has your father threatened you, Ms. Taylor?"

Dang it.

"He's not the most pleasant person," Harmony admitted, and wished she'd been able to avoid anything having to do with her father.

"I'm going to need his contact information as well. And the type of car he drives."

Harmony gave the detective her address and phone

number in Iowa. Then told him her father drove a huge white Ford truck.

"Okay, I think that's everything. I'll be in touch if we need anything else." The detective handed her his card and turned away, dismissing them. Not that she cared. Robert Nelson, per his card, wasn't too bad, but she'd rather be far away from him.

"There might be someone else to consider," Ry said.

The detective turned to face Ry. "And who would that be?"

Harmony wanted to know, too. Since she couldn't think of anyone else.

"I think his name is Harry Ericson. He's one of Harmony's bank customers and he threatened her earlier today. There were several witnesses to his outburst."

"No, Ry. He wouldn't do something like this. He's a sweet man going through a horrible time." Harmony jumped to Harry's defense. It was true he'd threatened her and how sad was it she believed he couldn't do this but that her father could?

"Do you have more information on Mr. Ericson?"

"At the bank. But it wouldn't be him. His wife is dying, and she's in the hospital. He wouldn't leave her."

"We have to check into all possibilities, Ms. Taylor. Chances are it was a group of teenagers with too much free time on their hands."

The detective nodded and walked off. Harmony wished it was a bunch of teenagers, but deep down, she didn't believe it for a second. The other cars didn't have any damage. Just hers. It had to be on purpose. But why had she been singled out? And if it wasn't her father, then who? She refused to believe it could be Harry.

9

"Your father could have done this?" Ry asked as soon as the detective was out of hearing range. To say he was furious was an understatement. Harmony hadn't been kidding when she said they didn't know each other. His family was amazing, loving, and supportive. He couldn't imagine ever thinking anyone in his family would set his vehicle on fire.

"Maybe. I don't know. But I'd believe it was him before Harry Ericson," Harmony replied as she wrung her hands.

Ry's gut churned with anger and worry for the shy, innocent woman who'd healed his cold, broken heart. Virginia Beach wasn't a large city, but from the sound of things, she'd come from a one-horse town or close to it.

"Will you tell me about him?" Ry tried to soften his voice. Harmony had been through enough for one evening. She didn't need him making it worse.

"I'd rather not, but I have a feeling you won't leave me alone until I do. Right?"

Ry smiled. She was scared, but not cowed—yet. "Yup,

you're right. You said we needed to learn about each other."

Harmony sighed before she answered, "Yes, that's true. I just hoped I wouldn't ever have to tell you about home."

"You won't scare me away if that's what you're worried about," Ry said gently. Then he pulled her against his side. He'd quickly become addicted to her touch. Her scent.

Her beautiful violet eyes searched his face. He didn't know what she was looking for, but she must have found it. "Okay. But can we do it inside? I really don't want to keep looking at my poor car."

"Sure. And you can pack a bag while we chat."

"Umm, what? Why would I do that? My car burned up, not my apartment," Harmony demanded.

"I don't think you should stay here alone until they figure out who did this. You're not safe. Whoever it is knows what kind of car you drive and where you're living." Ry didn't plan on backing down. If she didn't want to stay with him, he'd call one of her friends and she could stay with them.

"While I appreciate you worrying about me, I think you're taking this too far," Harmony said as she headed toward her unit.

"Are you sure?" Ry asked, pointing at her door.

Someone had taped a note made from torn pieces of a newspaper to her door.

I warned you. You took everything from me. Let's See how you like it when you've lost everything too.

. . .

"Still think it's not Harry Ericson, sweetheart?" Ry asked softly.

Harmony reached for the note to pull it off the door, but he stopped her. "You should probably call the detective. They are going to want to get fingerprints off it, and they'll take the note as evidence."

Ry hated to ruin her illusions about Harry. But when people lose everything, they change. He'd seen it often enough behind the wire. With every instinct he had, he believed Harry Ericson burned her car, and he wasn't giving the guy a chance to get close to Harmony. No fucking way.

While Harmony called the detective, Ry called Josh.

"What's up, fucker? I thought you'd be bumping uglies by now." Josh Hartman was a crude bastard, but he'd trust him with his life and Harmony's.

"Always the fucking asshole. There was an incident at Harmony's apartment—"

"What happened?" Josh was instantly all business, and that's what Ry counted on.

"Someone torched Harmony's car. Total loss. Police are on scene." Ry gave his friend the basics. He could fill the rest in after his team got there.

"Suspects?" Josh asked.

That was the tricky one. Ry believed it to be the local threat, but the wildcard was her father. And it was the wildcard that always bit them on the ass. But he also knew Harmony wouldn't want everyone to know her business.

"Probably the bank customer I told you about earlier, but there might be another tango."

"Fuuuuuccccckkkk." Josh's exclamation said it all. "I'll call Q and fill him in. What's the address?"

Ry rattled it off and disconnected as Harmony hung

up with Detective Nelson and walked into his embrace. He'd do anything to make everything disappear, but reality had other ideas. The shock of the last hour was taking its toll on her. The color had drained from her face, leaving her pale and fragile looking. Her lips were tight with tension and her eyes red-rimmed from her tears. Frustration that he couldn't fix this for her increased his tension. While the need to protect her made him tighten his hold on her.

Her frame seemed smaller now, and as she shuddered against his chest, it was like being kicked in the gut. "Everything will be okay, I promise," Ry murmured, hoping to ease some of her worry and Whiskey nudged her hand. His wet nose startled her.

Harmony sniffled, and when she looked up at him, tears pooled in the depths of her violet eyes that had turned into deep pools of sorrow. "It will never be okay. How can it? It's all changed, and if it was Harry, then I'm responsible."

"But it will be, and you're not alone to deal with this. You have me, my team, and your friends. Harry made his choices. You didn't force him to take the loan or put his house up as collateral. You didn't give his wife cancer. It's a series of horrible events. And I feel for him, but *he* made the wrong choices. You. Did. Nothing. Wrong."

"It doesn't feel that way to me," Harmony said as she buried her face against his chest.

The crime scene techs showed up with Detective Nelson. Relieved, Ry could finally move her away from the door and the offensive note. As hard as it was for Harmony to stay there, he wanted to make sure no one touched anything.

"Ms. Taylor, how about we go back over to my car, and we can talk some more?" Detective Nelson asked.

"Can't we go inside my apartment?" Harmony replied as she turned in Ry's arms to face the detective.

"It's a crime scene, at least out here. Until they're finished, you can't go inside. And we'll want to check the interior to make sure no one is inside."

Ry had already known the answer before she'd asked it. She looked so fragile, although she had a steel backbone. Instead of falling apart, she stiffened her spine and nodded. Even though he'd bet that all she wanted was to run and get as far away as possible.

"Do you have a bottle of water in your truck?" Harmony asked as they headed toward the detective's car.

"No, but I called Josh and the guys are bringing some water and whatever else they can think of," Ry said and squeezed the hand the clung to his. Then he looked down at Whiskey. He'd stayed near her on her right, making sure she was safe. He couldn't have asked for a better wingman.

"We won't allow your team inside the tape," Detective Nelson stated.

"I didn't expect it. We're aware of what we can and can't do on US soil," he responded. He was sure the detective had run his ID and knew he was a SEAL. Ry's visceral need to protect his woman wouldn't interfere with any legal investigation. But it didn't mean he wouldn't try to figure out what the fuck was going on.

When they reached the detective's car, he opened the driver's door for Harmony. "How about you sit down while we talk? I promise I won't arrest you. But you're exhausted, and I'd rather not give your boyfriend an excuse to punch me."

Ry understood the detective, recognizing him as another protector, but no way in hell would he or any of his team ever lay hands on anyone in law enforcement except to save them.

Harmony gave him the ghost of a smile, sat down, and promptly fell against the horn. Ry felt for Harmony, knowing how she hated to be the center of attention. She'd blame it on her clumsiness. Her exhaustion was obvious. Her day had been wall-to-wall stress. It surprised him she hadn't tripped all evening. Maybe holding her hand had helped to keep her steady.

"Thank you for that. I know everyone is awake now," Detective Nelson said with a grin.

"Umm, you're welcome. I think? I'm not sure anyone needed to hear that," she added.

Ry could have hugged the guy when Harmony smiled up at them.

"Trust me, it's not the first time that's happened. But let's get these questions taken care of so you can get some rest."

"Sounds good," Harmony answered.

Ry and Whiskey stood next to the car, close enough to close ranks around her if needed.

"So, what else can you tell me about the bank customer? His name is Harold Ericson, correct?"

Harmony nodded and took a deep breath. "Yes, that's his name. His wife's name is Barbara, and the doctors diagnosed her with a virulent form of lung cancer. He needed money for the hospital bills. They were my first customers when I transferred to this branch."

Nelson made some notes, but only a few. Ry suspected that he'd already learned most of the information. "Okay, so you approved their loan?"

"Oh no. I don't have the authority for that. I'm a customer relationship manager, so I answer questions and help with accounts, things like that. Harry had already maxed out his credit cards and couldn't get a personal loan, so I suggested using his house as collateral."

"But you don't approve the loans?"

"No, the underwriters do somewhere offsite. I just helped him complete the paperwork and submit it."

"Got it. And why did he go see you earlier?

"Because he got the foreclosure papers. When he failed to make his payments, the bank started the foreclosure process. I didn't know until he showed me the papers this morning." Harmony wrung her hands as she answered the questions. As he watched her tension increase with every question, Ry ached to wrap her in his arms and whisk her away.

Then his phone buzzed in his pocket. His team had arrived and was waiting by his truck.

"Hey, Josh is here. Is it okay if I go grab a bottle of water for Harmony?" he asked the cop. Then he turned to Harmony. "Do you need anything else? Are you cold? I can grab one of my sweatshirts if you'd like."

She gave him a half-smile and nodded. "Oh yes, please. That would be great, thank you."

"I'll be right back. Whiskey, you stay with Harmony and keep her safe."

The dog woofed and sat in front of her. Ry nodded. No one would get by him. "They'll let me back through the tape, right?"

"Yes, you'll be able to get back through," Nelson responded.

Not caring what anyone thought, he kissed Harmony on her forehead and squeezed her shoulder. He hated to leave her even for a few minutes, but he didn't have any other options.

"I won't be long," he promised, and then headed toward the other side of the parking lot where his team was waiting.

Ry expected his teammates to be waiting by his truck, but he was surprised to see Rafe and Ryan from the Black Eagle team, too.

"The gang's all here," Josh joked as Ry approached the group.

"Josh told us what he knew. Anything else you can share?" Quinn asked.

"My gut is telling me it's Ericson, especially after seeing the note hanging on her door. But when the detective asked Harmony about any suspects, her first thought was her father."

"What the fuck?" Fergus sounded as shocked as the rest of them looked.

"Yeah, that's pretty much what I thought. All I know so far is that she's from Norwalk, Iowa. From what she's said, it's one of those towns where everyone knows each other."

"I'll see what Chrissy can dig up. She still has lots of connections in the FBI," Ryan said.

"Thanks, bro. I appreciate you both being here."

"Are you kidding me? Have you met my wife, the spitfire?" Rafe grinned.

"Yeah, and the only reason Chrissy isn't here is that she got called in on something," Ryan said.

"Harmony will appreciate knowing she has lots of friends now. From the few things she's mentioned, I think she's spent most of her life being alone." If he had his way, she'd never be alone again.

"That fucking sucks," Luca Rossi said. "I guess it's a good thing she's one of us now. Right?" Then he looked over at Ry for confirmation.

"Yeah, she's one of us, even if she doesn't know it yet."

The others nodded.

"What do you need us to do?" Quinn asked.

"The police are tracking down Ericson. If it's him, they should catch him before he does anything else. But I think we need to look at her past. Figure out what the deal is with her father and her ex-boyfriend. I'm hoping she'll tell me, but if her father is behind this, I'm not sure we should wait."

"You know the shit is going to hit the fan when she finds out, right?" Josh said.

"Yeah, probably, but hopefully she'll understand why we did it," Ry answered, and prayed he was right. If he lost Harmony because he needed to keep her safe, he could live with that. Maybe.

"We've got your six," Fergus said.

"I never doubted it." Ry grinned at his friends and teammates. They would always be there for each other without question. "I need to get back to Harmony. I promised I'd be quick."

"Let me get the water from my truck. I grabbed some protein bars too. I wasn't sure how long you guys would be with the cops."

"Thanks, I'm not sure either. But I'm not letting her sleep here even if they let her into her apartment," Ry said as he unlocked the truck and reached into the back to grab a sweatshirt out of his go-bag.

"She can stay with us if she doesn't want to stay with you," Rafe suggested.

"Thanks, I might have to take you up on that. We'll see. I'm hoping she'll stay with me. Maybe Whiskey can convince her. She loves that dog." Ry grinned.

"He's a hell of a lot more lovable than you are, fucker," Josh added.

"That's the truth, too," Luca said with a grin.

"Yeah, yeah. Enjoy your fun while it lasts. Payback's a

bitch. All right, I need to get back to Harmony. I'll call if I find out anything."

"Don't forget to text us the note. And we'll let you know what we find out," Quinn said, and thumped Ry on the back.

"Thanks, I really appreciate it. Sorry to drag you all out here. I thought I'd have more information."

Josh handed him a bag with a six-pack of water bottles and the protein bars. "No problem, you'd do the same for any of us. Just take care of your woman."

"You know I will." Ry liked how that sounded. His woman. Now he just had to convince her.

As soon as Ry reached Harmony's side, the detective excused himself and walked over to one of the other officers.

"Is everything okay," Ry asked as he draped his hoodie over Harmony's shoulders and handed her a water bottle.

"Yes, I think he was afraid to leave me alone. But I have Whiskey and couldn't be safer," she answered and leaned forward to hug his dog.

If Ry hadn't been watching, she would have pitched headfirst onto the asphalt parking lot. She'd misjudged the distance and lost her balance. But he caught her before she hit the ground.

She looked at him ruefully. "Dang. I am in full-on klutz mode now."

"No, sweetheart, you're just exhausted and probably a little scared," Ry said gently.

Whiskey licked her face and leaned against her too.

"I can't stop thinking about what would have happened if I'd been home alone when all of this happened."

"But you were safe with an entire team and a half of SEALs. I don't think you can get much safer than that."

"Very true. And don't forget the Krav Maga queen.

Chrissy could take out all of you," Harmony said, then drained the water bottle. "Gosh, I can't believe I'm so thirsty."

"I seriously doubt she could take out all of us. We're highly trained and lethal. Besides, Ryan has been studying it to keep up with her," Ry said as he reached into the bag to grab another water bottle and hand it to Harmony. Josh had been smart to bring a six-pack since he didn't know if they'd be there for a while or if Detective Nelson would ask them to meet him at the station.

A few moments later, the detective returned. "I think we have all we need for now. If I need anything else, I'll call you. In the meantime, be vigilant until we catch whoever did this. If you feel threatened, call me. Don't hesitate, just do it. If you can't find my card, dial nine-one-one. Okay?"

"Yes, sir. Thank you. Does this mean I can get into my apartment?"

"I'm afraid not, it's still a crime scene. But Officer Roberts will let you inside to pack a bag. We should have it cleared sometime tomorrow."

"But..."

"It's okay, Harmony, we'll figure it out. Let's go grab your things," Ry said.

Her eyes narrowed as they searched his face. But she slowly stood without tripping and they followed the officer to her apartment. She'd already given them her keys so they could check it out, and the door was still open.

Ry and Whiskey stood near the door and watched as the officer followed her into the apartment. It didn't look like anyone had been in there since he'd picked her up earlier, and for that, he was grateful. This was hard enough for Harmony without having everything she owned destroyed. Though, if Ericson had the chance to do it, Ry believed he would.

What he didn't understand was what had triggered the guy. He'd been pissed off earlier, but this was some next-level shit. They needed to find out what had happened between the time when he'd left the bank earlier and this evening when he torched Harmony's car.

10

Harmony grabbed her suitcase out of the bedroom closet. Even though Detective Nelson said she could probably come home tomorrow, she didn't want to take any chances. Money was tight, and she didn't want to have to go clothes shopping just to go to work.

Knowing better than to grab more than one outfit at a time didn't stop her from doing it. It only took three steps from the closet before she landed on the floor on top of her clothes. Gawd. And, of course, the officer witnessed the entire thing.

"Do you need help, ma'am?" he asked politely.

Her cheeks burned with mortification as she imagined him recounting the story at work the next day and his fellow officers laughing until they cried.

"I'm fine. But thank you for offering." It's not like this stuff didn't happen all the time to her. But it was always worse when there were witnesses. But at least he hadn't grabbed her by the arm and dragged her off the floor like her father used to. He'd dislocated her shoulder more than once over the years.

She did her best to look graceful as she pulled herself and her dresses off the floor. She folded them neatly and tucked in a pair of dress shoes. Then she grabbed two pairs of jeans and a couple of sweaters since it was getting cooler in the evenings. Saving her underwear for last, she was trying to figure out how to get them out without the officer seeing her plain cotton granny panties and matching bras. No sexy lingerie for her—at least not yet, anyway.

The officer sighed from the doorway. She was taking too long to pack, but the more she rushed, the more anxious she became. Where would she go, how would she get around without a car? Worry weighed heavily on her shoulders. She just wanted to climb into her bed and pull the covers over her head.

"Ma'am, you need to hurry." He sounded aggravated. Probably wished he was anywhere but there.

"I'm trying. I just need to grab a few more things," Harmony answered. Giving up on trying to hide her unmentionables, she pulled a couple of her nightshirts out of a drawer and then wrapped them around her bras and panties. Then shoved all of it into her suitcase. She was sure she was forgetting something, but all the stress was making it hard for her to focus.

"Just need to grab a few things from the bathroom, then we can go," Harmony said as she slid past the officer to get her toothbrush and other toiletries. After shoving them into the suitcase, she glanced around the room for anything she might have missed. It was a good thing, too, since her makeup bag was still sitting on the dresser.

Harmony felt like a homeless waif, being evicted onto the street with nothing but her suitcase and the clothes on her back. Was this how Harry felt?

As soon as Ry saw her, he wrapped her in his

embrace so she was nestled snuggly against his muscled chest. She struggled at first, but then gave in to his warmth and inhaled his woodsy, male scent, and listened to the steady beat of his heart. His comforting embrace soothed her frayed edges, and the world didn't seem so bleak.

"C'mon let's get you away from here," Ry murmured as his cheek rested against her head.

"I don't have anywhere to go." She hated how desolate she sounded.

"Yes, you do, sweetheart. Several options, really. We'll discuss it when we get back to my truck. Okay?"

"Okay," Harmony mumbled against him.

"That's my girl." Ry released her and picked up her suitcase from where she'd dropped it. Then he took her hand in his, twining their fingers together. As soon as he'd stepped back, she missed the comfort of his arms. But holding his hand helped keep her anxiety at bay.

As they made their way through the parking lot, she noted the lack of crowds. It was an enormous relief. Harmony had feared it would be worse than earlier, but the boredom of the scene seemed to have taken its toll. There were still a few hangers-on—some may have been her neighbors, but she wouldn't recognize them if they were. Mostly, it was easy to see that her father wasn't in the crowd, and neither was Harry.

Ry opened the door of the truck. Whiskey jumped in first, then he helped Harmony get settled. Instead of getting in on the driver's side, she watched Ry walk the perimeter of the truck first, and she wondered if he was looking for something. Then he put her suitcase and the plastic bag with the water bottle into the small area behind his seat.

Ry started the engine and turned the heat on low. Then

he turned to her. "Well, Ms. Taylor, it would seem you are in great demand."

"What do you mean? Demand for what, exactly?" Had Detective Nelson changed his mind about letting her leave?

"I just meant that you get to make a choice on where you'd like to stay. Meghan has invited you to stay with her, but I'd prefer it if you'd stay with Whiskey and me at my apartment. And before you object, I have a spare bedroom. You'd have your privacy."

"Meghan wants me to stay with them? How does she know I need a place to stay?"

"When I texted Josh to have him bring the water, he let the team know. They were still at the Ready Room, so Rafe and Ryan came too."

"You shouldn't have done that. It's bad enough you're caught up in this mess now," Harmony said. The last thing she wanted was their pity or for them to feel obligated to help.

This had been her chance to start over, to be strong, to stand on her own two feet and prove to herself that she could do whatever she wanted. But here she was just a few months later—homeless, with no transportation, and she'd have to rely on her new friends for help. Just thinking about it made her want to throw up. Karma must really hate her.

"Sweetheart, whatever you're thinking, just stop. You're part of our family now. I know it's soon, probably way too soon for this conversation. But in my heart, I know we're meant to be together."

"But—" Harmony tried to interrupt him, but he stopped her.

"No, please let me finish."

She nodded. The sincerity in his deep blue eyes tugged on her heartstrings, and the butterflies were in full flight in her stomach. Oh, how she wanted to believe him, but it was too soon. He didn't know her secrets.

"I believe sometimes things just happen. And when I met you, the last thing I was looking for was a relationship. But it was like being struck by lightning."

"No, that was the calamity curse," Harmony murmured.

"Cute, but no, sweetheart. Sorry. I'm only telling you so you don't think you're causing trouble by needing help. You've been through hell tonight, and probably for a long time from the little you said about your father. But you're in a safe zone now. Even if you don't want a relationship, you're still part of our family."

Harmony didn't know what to say. "I… you." She shook her head and started over. "I've never had this kind of support before. I don't know how to thank you." Tears welled up in her eyes and she brushed them away with the back of her hand. She was tired of being weak. Pulling herself together, she straightened her shoulders and met Ry's gaze.

"You don't have to thank me. I wouldn't want it any other way," Ry replied with a gentle smile. The corners of his eyes crinkled, and she wanted to reach over and run her hand over his cheek. "So, where would you like to stay?"

Harmony took a deep breath. It was time to grab what she wanted and not worry about what anyone else thought. "I'd like to stay with you and Whiskey. If you're sure you don't mind?" She waited for his reaction and when he smiled, she released the breath she'd been holding, and the butterflies in her tummy settled.

"Are you kidding? I'm ecstatic. Did you hear that, Whiskey? She's coming to stay with us." There was no mistaking the excitement in Ry's voice.

Whiskey woofed, and then with one lick covered half her face with a slobbery kiss.

Giggling, she hugged the big German shepherd and smiled at Ry. The tightness in her shoulders eased, as she relaxed for the first time in hours.

"I'm glad I went grocery shopping earlier, or we'd have to go now," Ry said. "Although I don't have a lot of breakfast food."

"That's okay. I just have coffee in the morning." Harmony stopped eating breakfast years ago. No breakfast meant less time around the Kraken—the secret name she used for her father.

"I have coffee and a protein bar or shake. Especially if I have PT."

"Oh, right. Didn't Quinn say you have to be on base for seven am?" If Ry left that early, she'd need to call for an Uber to get to the bank on time. The drive-thru opened at eight, but the rest of the employees didn't need to be in before that. But it would take time to drive across town to the bank and then all the way out to the base. He'd never make it on time for PT.

"Nope, he told me I didn't have to report tomorrow. So, I owe you one now, because you got me out of PT." Ry glanced over at her, probably to see her reaction.

"You don't owe me anything, Ry. I'm the one who will owe you big time. Quite the first date, huh?"

Whiskey nuzzled her arm and whimpered, and she realized she'd been wringing her hands. The dog was more intuitive than most of the humans she knew.

"That's for sure. I don't think either of us will ever forget it."

"Yup, I agree. Do you think we'll ever have a normal evening? Dinner, or a movie, and no extra hysteria involved?" It really was ridiculous. First Harry at the bank, and then the car. No way was she going to ask the universe what else could happen. She knew it would delight in showing her.

"We definitely will, sweetheart. And at the end, you'll probably think it was the most boring date you've ever had."

"I sincerely doubt it. Boring might be nice. I'm a stay-at-home type of girl. Reading or a movie is fine with me." Harmony watched his profile to figure out what he was thinking. He was probably ready to take back his earlier words, and she hadn't even gotten to the messy stuff yet.

A few minutes later, they pulled into Ry's apartment complex, and knots formed in her tummy. Even though he said she'd have her own room, it was the first time she'd be spending the night with anyone besides her father. It sure was a night of firsts.

"I need to take Whiskey for a walk before we go inside. Do you want to wait here or come with us?" Ry asked as he hopped out of the truck.

"I'll come." She'd expected Whiskey to jump out the door as soon as Ry opened it, but he waited for her to get out and then jumped down beside her.

Ry reached into the glove box and grabbed a plastic bag and then attached Whiskey's leash. "We just walk over here at night. Although sometimes he likes to go for a run. But he's tired from the mission, too."

"Awww. I didn't think about that. You must be exhausted." She barely knew this man, and yet he'd been more protective of her than anyone she'd ever met.

"I'm fine. I slept some on the plane, and this is nothing compared to some of our missions. We're lucky to get more than a few minutes of rest at a time."

"I don't know how you do it. But I'm so glad there are men like you who put their lives on the line for the rest of us." The heat rose in Harmony's cheeks at the heat in his expression.

"Most of us couldn't imagine doing anything else," Ry said as they walked hand-in-hand around the complex waiting for Whiskey to take care of business.

"Did you always want to be a Navy SEAL?" Harmony asked.

"Not at first. But after nine-eleven I knew I wanted to defend my country."

"You were young, though." Harmony figured he couldn't be that much older than her.

"I was eleven. But I don't think my parents believed me when I told them I wanted to join the marines. They always figured I'd work in the family business. I would have, if I hadn't found out about the SEAL teams."

Harmony couldn't imagine having a conversation like that with the Kraken. It was his way or no way. She'd earned a scholarship to the University of Iowa, but he wouldn't let her take it. She ended up going to the local college and then he arranged for her job at the bank.

Before Harmony moved to Virginia, she often wondered if her mother hadn't run off if her life would've been different. She'd cried for her at first, then prayed she'd come back for her, but it never happened. Not that she blamed her for leaving with the way her father acted, but she couldn't understand why she'd left Harmony behind.

"What are you thinking about so hard?" Ry asked.

She got the feeling it wasn't the first time he'd asked her a question. "Just thinking about home. Your family sounds wonderful."

"They are. If I can get the time off, I'm going up there for Thanksgiving. I'd like to take you with me."

"Ry…"

"Don't say no. It's still a few months away. You have plenty of time to decide." He looked at the dog. Now that Whiskey finished his business, we'll grab your bag and get you settled."

Ry led her upstairs to his apartment. When he opened the door, Whiskey pushed past him and disappeared inside.

"Is something wrong?" Harmony asked.

"Not at all. He goes through the apartment and makes sure there's no threat."

"Oh. Aren't you worried about hurting anyone inside?"

"No, they shouldn't be in my home. If they're inside, they are the ones who should worry. Whiskey will take them down and wait for me to come to him."

"Like the police dogs on the news?"

"Very similar, except he's protecting his teammates," Ry said proudly.

"Maybe I should get a dog," Harmony mused. "I'll have to check my lease and see if they're allowed."

A moment later, Whiskey returned, and Ry reached inside, flipped a switch to turn on the lights, and pushed the door open wider to give her room to go inside.

"After you, sweetheart. This is your home for as long as you'd like," Ry said as she walked into the apartment.

Harmony didn't respond, just looked around at his bachelor pad. It fit him. The light beige walls almost exactly matched the wall-to-wall carpet. He had a brown leather couch in the living room facing the largest TV she'd ever seen. It hung on the wall, and below it was a table with a video game console.

There was a coffee table in front of the couch. Next to

that was a huge floor cushion. Probably Whiskey's bed. A desk with a laptop and printer was in the far corner of the room, opposite the sliding glass doors onto a balcony.

The apartment was an open floor plan, and an island separated the living room from the kitchen. It had lots of cabinets and stainless-steel appliances. To the right of the kitchen was a long hallway.

"You have a lovely place," Harmony said. Her apartment was much smaller, but perfect for her, and the first place she'd ever called her own.

"Thank you. I should probably do some decorating, but I'm not here all that much. Want to see your room?"

"Yes, please. I'm sure you want to get some sleep," Harmony said as she followed him down the hallway with Whiskey on her heels.

"I was hoping we could talk for a bit. Unless *you're* too tired?" Ry said as he opened the door to the bedroom that would be hers.

Harmony couldn't have been more surprised when she followed him into the room. Since it was his spare room, she hadn't expected more than a bed and maybe a table with a lamp. But there was a queen-sized bed with a rose floral comforter and lots of pillows. The nightstands matched the headboard and the triple dresser. It looked like a fancy hotel room.

"You decorated this room?" Harmony asked.

Ry laughed. "Nope, can't take credit for this. When my sister came down to visit, she did it. It was easier to let her than argue about it. Charli is something else. But I think you'll really like each other."

"Her name is Charlie?"

"It's her nickname, C-H-A-R-L-I. Her real name is Charity. But she can't stand it. When she started middle school, she told everyone she would only answer to Charli."

"And your parents didn't mind?" Harmony couldn't even fathom getting away with that.

"Nope. My father hates it too, but it's a family name on my mom's side. Mine is too. But it's not as bad as hers." Ry chuckled.

The deep rumble in his chest warmed her insides and raised goosebumps on her arms. "I like your name. I've never heard it before, but it suits you."

"Thank you, ma'am. The bathroom is the next door over. My room is at the end of the hall. There's a master bath, so you have this one all to yourself. Get settled and come out to the living room when you're done. I'm going to make some popcorn."

Ry stepped into the hallway, but Whiskey didn't budge from her side. "C'mon, buddy. Let's give Harmony some space." But the dog still didn't move, and Harmony giggled.

"It's okay, he can stay. I don't mind."

"If he gets in your way, just kick him out."

11

Ry grabbed a beer out of the fridge and took a swig as he leaned against the island while he watched the bag of popcorn fill with air and listened for the kernels to pop. It had been a hell of a day, but he'd protected his woman and now she was safe in his apartment, for now. If the note hadn't been on her door, he doubted she'd have agreed to stay with him. He'd avoided that issue. But now he had to convince her to tell him about her father.

The popping started as his cell buzzed in his pocket. Josh.

"Hey, bro. How's it going? Any news?" Ry asked.

"Nothing yet. I wanted to check on your status," Josh replied. It was like they were still on a mission.

"I'm at home. Harmony came with me, and she's getting settled in the spare room."

"What's that noise?"

"Popcorn. I figured Whiskey deserved a treat after everything."

"Fuck yeah. That dog is worth his weight in gold. What

a clusterfuck. He pulled our asses out of the fire," Josh said with a sigh.

"No shit. When I see Rick, I'm going to kick his fucking ass. That was the worst intel we've ever received. Motherfucker," Ry said angrily. It had been a close call, and if not for Whiskey, they'd have lost Luca.

"You and me both. What is the point of having a CIA liaison if what he gives us is FUBAR?"

"I wish I knew. Too bad we can't work with Chrissy more often. She usually nails it." Ry loved it when Chrissy supplied the intel. She had an innate sense of things and could see patterns where no one else could. Of course, Ryan, her fiancé, really hated it when she went behind the wire with any of the teams.

"Did you get any info about the father yet?" Josh asked. He'd changed the subject before they both got too pissed off.

"Not yet—" Ry stopped when he heard Whiskey's patter come into the kitchen and smiled. The call of the popcorn. It worked every time.

"Josh, I gotta go. Let me know if you hear anything."

"Copy that. I'll just be sitting here thinking of ways to torture my neighbor. She messed with my yard again."

Ry laughed. "I'm sure you'll come up with something that will piss her off." This was an ongoing battle ever since Tempest—and for the life of him, he couldn't remember her last name—moved into the house next to Josh's last year. The two fought like cats and dogs over every little thing. No one on the team had met her, but from the stories Josh shared, she lived up to her name.

"You know it. She won't know what hit her." Josh chuckled.

"Good luck with that. Later." Ry shoved the phone

back into his pocket. When he looked up, Harmony was leaning against the other side of the island, watching him.

Harmony looked so young as she eyed him quizzically. She'd removed her makeup, and with her hair in a ponytail and wearing yoga pants and a T-shirt, she looked more like a college student than a grown woman.

"Everything okay?" Harmony asked.

"Yeah, Josh called to make sure you were okay and to whine about his neighbor. She makes him crazy, and he does everything he can to annoy her right back," Ry answered. He hated not telling her they were looking into her father, but he refused to take chances with her safety.

"That doesn't sound like a peaceful home environment," Harmony said.

"No, it doesn't. I wouldn't want to come home and deal with it. There are some advantages to apartment living."

"Yes, and even with the lease, it's a finite amount of time to have an annoying person."

"Exactly. Would you like something to drink? I have wine, beer, and water," Ry offered.

"Water would be wonderful. Thank you."

Ry grabbed a bottle of water from the fridge, loosened the cap, and gave it to Harmony. "You're welcome to anything that's here. Okay?"

"Are you sure? I can give you some money for groceries."

"I'm sure, and there's no need. I've got us covered."

The microwave dinged. Ry opened the door and pulled out the bag of popcorn. Whiskey sniffed the air and chased his tail in a circle and whined. Then he jumped up and put his two front paws on the island as he watched Ry pour the treat into a large bowl.

"Is he okay?" Harmony asked as she watched the dog's antics.

"Yeah." Ry chuckled. "He loves popcorn, and he gets it as a treat whenever we return from a mission. And since he was extra good today, he'll get a little more than usual."

"That's so cute. He's an amazing dog."

"Yes, he is." Then he grabbed the bowl of popcorn and his beer. "I'm hoping we can talk, but if you'd rather watch a movie, we can do that." Ry walked over to the couch and sat down, putting the popcorn on the table. Whiskey sat down next to him and rested his paw on his knee. Ry chuckled.

"I know you're waiting. But how about we let Harmony have some first since she's our guest?" Ry said to the dog.

Harmony followed them over to the couch but hadn't sat down. Her cheeks paled and her eyes darted around the room like she was looking for a way to escape. Ry knew she didn't want to talk about her father, but he didn't realize it would bring her this much anxiety.

"How about you pick a movie? They're all in the center drawer of the console table. I'm sure you're ready to unwind after the day you had, and we'll talk tomorrow."

"I like that idea. Relaxing to a movie sounds great," Harmony replied, as the strain around her lips eased and she smiled.

She had a hard time picking one, but mostly because they were all action movies. Not a chick flick in the pile, and Ry made a mental note to order some on Amazon. When she finally decided, she surprised him again with her choice, picking the first Bourne movie.

"Do you know what this is about?" he asked as he popped it into the Blu-ray player.

"Yes, I read all the books. It was the one thing I had control over," Harmony answered.

Ry wondered if she even realized how much that one sentence told him about her life back in Iowa. The need to ask her about her father was like an itch he couldn't scratch. The sheer amount of patience it took to not bug her about it would shock the shit out of Josh.

Whiskey moved to Harmony's side of the couch, and Ry laughed. His dog knew a soft touch when he met one. Sure enough, as soon as he flashed his big puppy dog eyes, Harmony melted.

"Do you have some kind of signal before Whiskey can have some popcorn?"

"Nope, no rules. He can have it anytime. More times than not, he'll jump onto my lap if I make him wait too long. Looks like he gave up on me and is trying his luck with you."

Harmony giggled. "I can give him some?"

"Sure. You can put a handful on the floor or toss them at him. He's great at catching."

"Cool," she said, then took a handful out of the bowl and tossed one at Whiskey. "Oh, you're right. He is fantastic at this," she remarked as she tossed kernel after kernel at the dog. He caught every one of them, even when she'd toss it high into the air.

This Harmony, the relaxed and smiling version, enchanted Ry. The movie was long forgotten as she continued to play with the dog. Ry delighted in her enjoyment, as did the grateful and soon to be overstuffed canine.

"Did you have a dog when you were young?" It was an innocent question and just popped out of Ry's mouth while he watched her toss the puffed corn and Whiskey jump and run all over the room to catch them. It was also the perfect way to get her to talk about her life in Iowa—maybe.

"Nope, no dog. My father was very strict. There were no pets allowed. When I was five or six, I won a goldfish at the local fair. I was so excited, even though I knew that he probably wouldn't let me keep it. Sure enough, as soon as he saw it, he took the bag from me and flushed it down the toilet."

"You're kidding?" Anger and sympathy for the five-year-old Harmony gutted him. If the man had been there, he'd have put him in a world of pain. He couldn't imagine the heartlessness of her father.

"I wish. But nope, and then he punished me."

"Your father sounds like a real asshole. I'm sorry, but I don't understand how he could have treated you liked that, baby. No wonder you moved here." Ry's heart ached for her. He had to fight the desire to pull her onto his lap and kiss away the pain reflected on her face. Growing up in that house must have been a living hell.

"He isn't the most pleasant person," she admitted. She and Whiskey finished the popcorn, and the dog finally laid himself down in his bed. Ry had been lucky to get a couple of handfuls out of the bowl before it all went into the dog's belly. With a sigh, Harmony leaned against the other arm of the couch and wrapped her arms around her bent knees.

"No, it doesn't sound like it. You never mention your mother. Was she afraid to stand up to him?" Ry didn't want to push her, but he couldn't help himself when she gave him the opening.

"Well, more like the opposite. She left him and me. One day, she was just gone. I was pretty young. I used to wonder if that's why my father was so mean. But I think he was probably always this way, and that's why she left. I don't think I'll ever forgive her for not taking me with her, though."

"Damn, I wouldn't either. What kind of mother leaves a young child with someone like that?"

"Exactly. I used to pray every night when I went to bed that she'd come back to get me, but it never happened."

"Did you try to find her when you got older?"

"I never thought about it. Besides, I would've had to do it behind my father's back, and if he found out, it wouldn't have been pretty. Maybe if I'd married Jim, but it turned out he wasn't any better."

"What happened with Jim?" Ry asked, unable to help himself. It amazed him she'd turned out so sweet and caring after her childhood, and he was sure he didn't know the half of it.

Harmony turned her head to look at him and quirked one of her perfectly arched eyebrows. "I guess you've gotten me to talk about this, anyway, huh?"

"We don't have to. I didn't mean to push you."

"You didn't, not really. And about my ex, Jim? Hmm. I might have met him once at a party, but my dad picked him out for me. Insisted it was time for me to get married. I'm not sure what my father had to promise him to agree, but I'm sure it wasn't cheap. In the end, it wasn't enough, since a week before the wedding he ran off with a woman from his office."

"What the fuck?"

Harmony's laugh wasn't pleasant. "Pretty much. And of course, it was my fault. I'd obviously driven him away. Father was so livid, he punched me in the face. I had a heck of a shiner and stayed home from work for a few days."

"And no one ever said anything? Not your teachers? No one? They let him get away with it?" Ry's fists clenched just thinking about the beating he'd give her father. It was bad enough to hit a woman, but his own child? He'd teach the fucker a lesson. No woman should ever be touched in anger, only in love.

"Everyone is afraid of him. It's pretty much his town. He's been mayor for as long as I can remember. He controls everything. If I was five minutes late, he'd send the sheriff out looking for me."

"If he's got that much control, I'd bet he's breaking the law."

"Maybe? I don't know. I'm just glad I got away. It was sheer luck I saw this job on the bank's website and put in for the transfer. I don't know how I got away with it. But it's only a matter of time until he tracks me down and tries to take me back."

"There's no way I'll let that happen, sweetheart. He doesn't have any control here."

Harmony sniffed back tears and shook her head. The hopelessness in her eyes broke his heart. Then she wedged herself in the opposite corner of the couch like she was trying to disappear and every one of Ry's protector instincts went on high alert.

Reaching over, he lifted her onto his lap and wrapped his arms around her. He half expected her to be annoyed, but it was a risk he was willing to take to erase the haunted look in her eyes.

"Ry, is this part of the interrogation technique? Because I have to say, this might actually work," Harmony said.

"Oh yeah? I'll have to remember that." Ry grinned.

Her change in demeanor surprised him. It had to be a built-in defense mechanism kicking in. He wished it was real. This was the Harmony he'd fallen for, and yes, he'd fallen hard. It was kind of crazy. He knew it, but he wouldn't change it for anything. When he held her in his arms and inhaled her sweet, flowery scent, he felt complete. Cat had never made him feel this way, and he'd thought he loved her. But it hadn't come close.

"You should. I bet it would work on anyone."

"Maybe, but I only need it to work on you." Ry rested his cheek on the top of her head. "Is there anything else I should know?"

"Isn't that enough?"

"Oh hell, it's way more than enough. But if he is dirty, then I think we need to find out and put him away where he can't hurt you ever again."

"Trust me, you don't want to poke that bear. He'll find a way to make you suffer," Harmony said, and she stiffened against him, strung tighter than a violin.

"Sweetheart, I have connections too, and mine are legal. He won't be able to hurt me."

"Don't underestimate him. You don't know what he's capable of. The man not only wouldn't let me go away to school with a complete scholarship, but he planned each step of my life, even to the job I have. I didn't want to work in a bank."

"Maybe you can find something you'd rather do, now that you're away from him."

"I don't know. It's possible. I liked my job here until I found out what they did to Harry and Barb."

"Unfortunately, bad things happen to good people, and Harry made his choice. If he torched your car, he'll go to jail. I feel for him, I really do. But he went off the rails."

"We don't know that he did it. I still think it's probably my father," Harmony insisted.

"If he did it, we'll catch him, too. But from everything you've told me, it doesn't seem to be his style. He's more devious in his actions," Ry said.

"That's true. Except when he punched me in the face, he always did his best to make sure none of my bruises were visible. But I think he was just so furious when he found out about Jim that he just lost it," Harmony said.

"He should never have laid a hand on you, sweetheart. Never. And if I have anything to say about it, it won't happen again," Ry vowed. Rage surged through him as acid churned in his gut. The man would pay if it was the last thing Ry ever did.

At his words, Harmony seemed to melt against him. Whether it was exhaustion or relief Ry wasn't sure. She'd kept it all to herself for so long, he hoped it was relief that she could finally share some of it.

Ry tipped Harmony's chin up with his finger so he could see her face. Unshed tears filled her beautiful eyes. He wanted to kiss away her pain, erase the memories of her childhood and give her shiny new ones. "Are you okay?"

"Getting there. I kept all of that to myself for so long, convinced it was all my fault. That he hurt me because I was bad, that he controlled me because I didn't know any better. But forcing me to marry Jim was the last straw. I hated them both. But I suppose I should thank Jim, or I'd never have gotten away." Harmony met his gaze and shrugged her shoulders. "Don't they say that God doesn't give you more than you can handle?"

Ry nodded, he'd heard that often from his mother. "Yup, I might have heard that a time or two."

"Thank you, Ry. I didn't realize how much I needed to talk about it." Harmony lifted her hand and placed it on his cheek, looking at him in wonder. "I feel lighter, freer than I can ever remember. It's like I just got rid of a huge yoke weighing me down.

"You deserve so much better, sweetheart," Ry said.

Their gaze connected, and her pupils dilated as her breath hitched.

The need to kiss her overwhelmed his better judgment. He paused with his lips only inches from hers, giving her a chance to stop him. Then a slight smile tipped the edges of her lips as she closed the distance.

12

As their mouths came together, Harmony sighed as her tongue glided over his soft lips. Ry tasted of salt and beer, and she decided it was her new favorite flavor. Desire pooled low in her belly. She wanted more, needed to be closer. Her arms circled his neck. Her fingers slid through the hair at the base of his head.

"Open for me, sweetheart," he murmured.

When she did, his tongue slipped inside her mouth and swept against hers. She groaned and timidly responded, copying his movements. She'd read about kisses like this, but this was her first. *Holy cow.* Her nipples hardened and her panties dampened. Filled with need, she pulled him closer.

When he released her mouth, she opened her eyes and gazed at him in wonder. *When had I closed them?* The quick staccato of his heartbeat matched hers. Didn't that mean he wanted this as much as she did? So why had he pulled away? Was it because she didn't know what she was doing?

"Why did you stop? Did I do something wrong?" Harmony asked, searching his face for answers.

"Oh, baby, no way. Far from it. You did everything right. Can't you feel my hard cock against your thigh?"

Moving her leg, Harmony's mouth formed an "O" as she realized he was throbbing against her. A purely female sense satisfaction filled her, and she felt sexy for the first time in her life, even if she didn't know what she was doing. She'd made Ry so excited he moaned, and it made her feel smug, until his lips claimed hers again and she couldn't think of anything but him.

Her toes curled as Ry's hand skimmed the side of her breast through her T-shirt and he kissed a path from her lips over her jaw and to her neck. Leaning her head back to give him better access, he nuzzled against her, then nipped her where her neck and shoulder met, sending more wetness into her panties.

"You're killing me, woman."

"I'm sorry," she stuttered.

"No, baby. It's a good thing." His smile melted the frozen places in her heart.

He took her breath away, and she didn't know how she'd gotten so lucky. Nothing in her life prepared her for the desire coursing through her veins. Were these feelings normal? She was probably the only twenty-eight-year-old virgin in the state of Virginia. It should embarrass her, but after everything she'd been through, it was pretty low on the list. She'd tried to masturbate a few times when she'd still been living at home, but she'd been too afraid her father would walk in and catch her.

Romance books were new to her, and she loved them. They'd kept her from feeling so lonely. At home, she'd only read what her father allowed. But one of the first things she'd done after getting settled was to download the Kindle app and a bunch of romances. She'd never been so turned on in her life. When she took her shower, she used her fingers to get off. Running her hands over her body, tweaking her nipples, and then sliding her fingers between her legs. She'd been so wet it only took a few strokes on her clitoris to send her over the edge.

It had felt good, and she'd been more relaxed afterward, but there was no shattering into a million little pieces, or bright lights flashing in front of her eyes. Afterward, she'd wondered if she'd done something wrong, or maybe it hadn't been a true orgasm. Not that she had anyone to ask.

But Ry's kisses. *Oh. My. God.* Everywhere he touched, her skin tingled, and she burned with need.

"Do we have to stop?" Harmony asked shyly. She was prepared to beg if necessary.

Ry ran his hand through her hair and across her cheek. "After everything you've been through, I'd feel like I was taking advantage of the situation."

"I don't care."

"You would tomorrow. I could kiss you all night, but it would lead to more. And I don't want you to have any regrets when we make love for the first time."

Harmony nodded. Ry was right, even if she didn't want to admit it. Was she ready to give her his virginity? Would he freak out about it? Or had he already figured it out?

"So, no more kisses?" Harmony asked.

"There will be plenty more, just not tonight. I think we need to get you to bed. What time do you need to be at work?" Ry asked as he stood with her in his arms and didn't release her until she was steady on her feet.

"I have to be there by eight, but I can call for an Uber."

"I don't have to be at PT at seven, so it's no problem to drop you off at work and head to base."

"Are you sure? You've already done so much for me." People helping was a new sensation for her. It would take some getting used to.

"I'm positive. Let's get you to bed." He took her hand and led her around the coffee table.

"I think I can figure out where it is," Harmony teased.

"Yes, I'm sure you can, but I love touching you. If it makes you uncomfortable—"

Harmony raised two fingers and put them over his lips. "It doesn't. I enjoy touching you, too. Unless you're worried that I'll fall on my face and sue you," she said.

Ry flashed her one of his one-hundred-megawatt smiles, then kissed her hand. "No, ma'am. Besides, I've already given you my most cherished possession… my heart."

Thank goodness he was holding her hand, because her heart flipped over, and all the blood rushed from her head. He'd mentioned earlier that he was falling for her, but could it be true? Did he see something in her she didn't see in herself? She hoped so, because she was almost positive that she'd fallen for him, too.

"I…I don't—"

"Sweetheart, there's no pressure here, honest. I learned a long time ago that waiting for the right time didn't always work out. I'm thirty-one years old and I know my mind and my heart. But if you're not there yet, or never get there, it's okay, too. You're stuck with me as a friend either way."

Harmony tried to hold back the tears that blurred her vision. Until Ry, she'd never known men could be kind and understanding. And he was all three, cubed. "You mean a lot to me, too." It felt lame after what he'd just said, but she had a lot of things to think about, and she needed to get through this mess with Harry or her father, or whoever it ended up being.

Ry stopped at the door of her room and kissed her gently on the lips like he'd just taken her home after a date, which he had—just not the way they'd planned on.

"I hope our next date is less eventful," Harmony said with a grin.

"You and me both. Sleep well. If you need anything, I'm just down the hall. Oh, I almost forgot. If you leave your door open, there's a good chance that Whiskey will invite himself in and onto the bed."

"Really? That would be so cool," Harmony exclaimed. "I hope he does."

Ry shook his head. "You don't know what you're asking for, but I guess you'll find out soon enough."

Harmony went into the bathroom first and brushed her teeth and washed up for bed. She'd left the bedroom door open and when she returned, Whiskey had made himself at home in the middle of the bed.

After tossing the extra pillows onto the chair in the corner, Harmony slid under the comforter. Whiskey moved over the slightest bit to give her enough room. Turning on her side, she cuddled against the dog and giggled. *My first bed partner would be huge, loyal, and covered in hair*. It wasn't Ry, but Whiskey seemed to be a good cuddler.

Ry checked on Harmony a half-hour later, and she was fast asleep, curled up with Whiskey. The big dog was the best judge of character he'd ever seen, and better than any FBI profiler he'd ever met. It made Ry wonder what would happen if either Harry or her father tried to hurt her. He was sure it wouldn't be pleasant.

Tired, but unable to sleep with all the thoughts running through his head, he got another beer from the fridge and turned on the news. More fighting had broken in Marikistan. Freedom fighters were trying to overturn the corrupt government. Nothing new really, it happened too often. He remembered hearing the name in a couple of their briefings, but he couldn't remember the specifics. Grabbing his phone off the table, he made a note to talk to Quinn about it when he saw him. None of the Red Falcons spoke the language, and it would help if at least one of them knew some if they ended up going in.

His phone was still in his hand when a text message popped up.

Josh: Any news on your end?

Ry: Learned more about the douchebag father.

Josh: Want to talk?

Ry: Not tonight. Harmony is already asleep. I'll be on base before nine.

Josh: No problem. Ryan talked to Chrissy. She's doing a deep dive into all parties.

Ry: She didn't have to deploy on a mission?

Josh: Nope. We got lucky. Or I guess Ryan did.

Ry: You are such a fucking asshole

Josh: And this surprises you? Wait till I tell you what happened with the bitch next door.

Ry: Did you ever try being nice to her?

Josh: Yes.

Ry: Didn't go well?

Josh: You could say that, since it's WWIII on our block now.

Ry: Did you see what's going on in Marikistan?

Josh: Yeah. Lots of fucked up stuff going on. I feel a trip coming up.

Ry: Yeah, me too. See you in the morning. Let me know if you hear anything before then.

Josh: Later.

There would be progress soon. He was sure of it. Especially since Chrissy was looking into the two suspects. If there was something to be found, she'd uncover it—it was her superpower.

The situation needed to be resolved soon. Ry didn't want this threat hanging over Harmony's head any longer than it had to. Hopefully, Detective Nelson would resolve the threat by arresting Harry. Except Ry's gut told him it was the father, even if he had nothing to prove it. It wouldn't be the first time his hunch had been correct.

The hairs on the back of Ry's neck twitched. Turning off the living room light, he peered around the edge of the vertical blinds covering the sliding glass doors. He couldn't be sure, but he thought he saw someone standing near the bushes at the edge of the property. It could be someone walking their dog, though it was after midnight. He wanted to go check it out, but he also didn't want to leave Harmony alone, even with Whiskey as protection. Then he checked again, but no one was out there now.

The lighting sucked on that part of the grounds, so Ry figured he'd check the area when he took Whiskey for a walk in the morning. Maybe he'd get lucky and find something pointing to one of the tangos.

It was late, and Ry was beat. He struggled to stay awake while watching an episode of *Jack Ryan.* After he'd nodded again, he gave in to the exhaustion and cleared away the beer bottles and popcorn remnants.

He stopped to check on Harmony and saw that Whiskey had moved to the bottom of the bed, but she was in the same place. A sliver of moonlight came through the curtains and made her blonde hair looked like spun gold on her pillow. With her face relaxed in sleep, she looked so young. From the information she'd given to Detective

Nelson, he knew she was twenty-eight. But in the moonlight, she could easily have passed for seventeen. Fighting the temptation to give her a kiss on her forehead, he went to his room and closed the door.

What he would have given to have her in his bed. He'd happily stay awake to make her come until she was boneless and happy next to him. But it wasn't the night for that. She'd wanted more, but he felt her indecision, too. When he'd first kissed her and she slid her tongue along his, he thought she might be a virgin, but when the kiss escalated, he wasn't sure. Either way, he'd coddle her. She deserved to be treated like a princess after the way the men in her life had treated her. There was no need to rush things.

13

It was almost quitting time, and Harmony couldn't wait for Ry to arrive. Sitting in her fishbowl of an office, she was restless and bored, even though she'd met with a few new clients. It had been too quiet for the last few days, with no sign of Harry or her father. Every day was the same—paperwork, the occasional client, and waiting for the day to end. She'd made enough paperclip chains to decorate a Christmas tree. Still, she'd take boring over being scared to death any day of the week. It made her consider what Ry mentioned about finding a job she'd enjoy.

Since Detective Nelson had yet to locate Harry, Ry talked Harmony into staying with him until they could be sure she'd be safe. She loved spending time with Ry, and as her personal Uber driver, she held off getting the rental car and saved a bunch of money. Unfortunately, Harmony couldn't stay with Ry forever, but she'd relish every moment they spent together.

After he dropped her at the bank every morning, he'd head to base and pick her up again around five. They'd pick up dinner on their way home. Harmony loved it, until she remembered it wouldn't last forever, but she'd enjoy it while it lasted.

When they finished eating, they'd walk Whiskey. Then they'd pick out a movie, but they rarely made it past the opening credits before Ry would lift her into his lap and kiss her senseless. She'd lose herself in him and nothing mattered except Ry—his kisses, his firm muscles rubbing against her hard nipples, and the softness of his chestnut brown hair as she tugged him closer.

"Harmony, may I have a word with you in my office?" Wendy Mercer, the branch manager, requested, then turned around and left.

Startled, she looked up from the paperwork she'd been rearranging on her desk. "Of course, I'll be right there." It seemed odd to Harmony. Why would Wendy want her to come to her office when she could have come in and sat down? But then Wendy Mercer did everything she could do to get ahead. From what Harmony had witnessed in just the few months she'd worked there, she didn't care who she hurt while she stepped on them on her way up the ladder.

Harmony tucked her cell phone into her dress pocket and went next door to her boss's office. Wendy had a phone to her ear when Harmony knocked on the open door. She waved her in and pointed to the chair opposite hers.

It made her feel awkward to wait while others were on the phone, like she was eavesdropping. She took her phone out and flipped through her apps while she waited. She'd only downloaded a few after she got the phone. It took some getting used to. Being a grown-up out in the real world wasn't anything like living in

Norwalk. Or maybe it was only her father who'd made it so different.

If she had her way, she'd never see William Taylor again, but she could count on one hand the number of times a wish had come true.

"Sorry about that," Wendy said after she disconnected the call. Then she opened a drawer in her desk and removed a file and put it down on her desk.

Harmony read her name on the file, and a sinking feeling slithered down her spine like a snake. Focusing on keeping her hands clasped in her lap instead of wringing them, she concentrated on remaining calm. She was dying to ask what was going on, but she kept quiet and waited.

"Harmony, I called you in here to let you know I'm adding a written warning to your employee file."

"Wait, a warning? For what?" Harmony's head pounded and her stomach churned. Searching her mind, she couldn't think of a thing she'd done wrong. She prided herself on being an excellent employee, following the rules, even if she didn't like them. Like with what they did to Harry and Barb. Or maybe that was it. They'd defaulted on their loan. She'd suggested they apply, so maybe it was that? But wouldn't the underwriters have the ultimate blame?

"There should be two, but since you didn't technically do anything wrong with the Ericson account, you're off the hook for that one."

What could she have done wrong? Harmony had only been at the bank for a few months. She kept to herself, did her job, and went home.

Wendy shuffled the papers in front of her, a delaying tactic Harmony recognized. "Your warning is for fraternization at work. You should know better, and if it happens again, you'll be terminated."

"I don't understand. When and who did I fraternize with?"

"The surveillance cameras recorded you kissing your boyfriend in front of the bank," Wendy said smugly.

"For that quick kiss?" Harmony exclaimed. Maybe a week ago she would have considered tit a kiss, but after spending the last few days in Ry's arms, making out on the sofa, there was no way it could be anything close to fraternization. She figure out why her boss would do this.

"Read your employment contract if you don't believe me," Wendy answered.

It was clear, that Wendy was enjoying herself, and Harmony still had no clue what she'd done to deserve her disdain.

Harmony wanted to rail at the woman, but she needed the job. Focusing on remaining calm, she said through gritted teeth, "I apologize, and it won't happen again."

"I hope not, Harmony. I'd hate to see you lose this job. Maybe you should make sure the big guy stays away from the bank, just in case."

Harmony nodded. "Is that all? Or is there something else you want to discuss?"

"Have you heard from that police detective? Are there any updates? We don't want any trouble here. The customers are our top priority," Wendy said.

"No, nothing yet. He said he'd call if there were any updates."

"Let me know if you hear anything," Wendy said and then picked up the phone.

Harmony couldn't get out of her office fast enough.

What a witch. But something bugged Harmony about the entire conversation. Why was Ry coming around an issue? If she said they couldn't kiss on bank property, he'd respect her wishes.

She was still contemplating Wendy's words when her cell phone rang.

"Harmony Taylor."

"It's me, sweetheart. Your chariot awaits, and so does your faithful steed," Ry said.

"My steed? I guess if I was a little shorter, I could ride Whiskey."

"Who said anything about Whiskey? I'm hoping you'll ride me," Ry replied and growled into the phone.

Gawd. Instant wet panties. She needed to do laundry or go by her apartment and pick up some more clothes, especially underwear. It was getting out of hand.

"You're horrible. I'll be right out," Harmony replied, her cheeks heating with embarrassment.

"We'll be waiting."

Harmony heard his chuckle as he disconnected. Darn. She'd fallen hard and way too fast. Hopefully, she could handle the heartbreak when it was over.

Checking her files, she finally found the employee handbook and her signed contract and tucked them in her purse. She checked her office and made sure she'd locked everything so Wendy wouldn't have an excuse to fire her. Then she walked out of her office and waved goodbye to Richard, the security guard, as he held the door open for her to leave.

As she stepped outside into the cool air, she inhaled deeply, ridding herself of her anger so it didn't taint her evening with Ry. They'd spent a wonderful four nights together, even if they hadn't made love yet, but when the police caught Harry, her fairytale would be over.

"Hello, beautiful," he called to her as she approached the truck, and Whiskey barked his greeting as he paced back and forth, waiting for her.

Ry got out to open her door and leaned down to kiss

her. When Harmony put up her hand to stop him, his expression clouded with worry.

"I'll explain in a minute," she said, seeing his hurt expression.

He nodded and closed the door when she buckled in.

As he pulled out of the parking lot, she saw him glance over at her as she received her requisite Whiskey licks.

"Did something happen today? Are you upset with me about the riding comment?" Ry asked.

"I'm not mad at you, not even a little. You are amazing and I've never been as happy as I am with you." She'd almost slipped and said the "L" word, but if he didn't feel the same, she didn't think she could handle it. Instead, she swallowed before continuing, "But yes, something happened at work today. I'm still trying to understand it all. Something doesn't feel right, and I have a bad feeling about it."

"Do you want to talk about it now or wait until we get home?" Ry asked.

His tone was different. Serious. He hadn't sounded like that since the night they torched her car. "Home, I think. Did something happen at your work today?"

"Yes, but it's nothing I can talk about. That's the hard part of my job, most of it's classified."

Harmony nodded. Her friends had warned her about this part. They said that the guys didn't have a choice, and they weren't deliberately locking the women out of their lives.

"I understand, no worries. What should we get for dinner tonight?" Harmony asked, changing the subject. Every night they'd had a different cuisine—Mexican, Italian, Mediterranean, Chinese—most of which she'd never tried before. Her father was a meat and potatoes kind of guy. She figured they had to be running out of countries soon.

"How about sushi? I bet you haven't eaten it before." Ry grinned.

"Umm, isn't that raw fish?"

"Yes, and no. Some of it's raw, but there's cooked sushi, too. They also have fried dishes called tempura. But I bet you'd like the sushi. What do you think?"

"Sure, why not. If I hate it, I'll make a PB&J."

Ry laughed. It was her standard response whenever he suggested something new.

"One of these days, I'll take you there to eat. It's really cool to see the chefs prepare your dinner in front of you."

"They do?"

"If you sit at the sushi bar, they do."

"There's a special bar for that?"

Ry chuckled. "Yes, but not like you're thinking. When we place our order, I'll show you."

The restaurant was almost empty, so they let Ry take her over to where the chefs worked on their dinner. They amazed her with the speed they created the beautiful little pieces of food. Ry ordered five rolls for him, and she picked out three cooked rolls. He also ordered edamame, steamed soybeans. They looked like peapods on steroids.

On their way out, Ry grabbed some chopsticks, promising to show her how to use them. Harmony had her doubts that she'd be able to pick up anything with two thin sticks, but he promised her she'd have fun trying. That was good enough for her.

Ry loved watching Harmony using or trying to use the chopsticks. After dropping rolls into the soy sauce and wasabi for the third time, she gave up. Watching her stab the roll with one stick like she was roasting marshmallows cracked him up.

"I don't know how you do that. You've got excellent chop sticking skills," Harmony said after poking another roll and dipping into the soy sauce.

"Chop sticking skills?" Ry laughed. "You invented a new word and I like it. We'll have to let everyone know about my mad chop sticking skills."

Harmony smiled as she chewed the roll that had barely fit into her mouth.

As much as she was enjoying dinner, he noted a sadness in her attitude that hadn't been there for the last few days. He couldn't wait to find out what had happened. It wasn't about Harry because Ry had checked in with Detective Nelson earlier, and they were still searching for the guy.

Harry Ericson had just disappeared, and no one could figure out where he'd gone. Ry worried that he might have taken his own life, especially when the detective informed him that his wife had passed away. It could have been the trigger that set him off. But after some things Chrissy discovered, Ry wasn't sure.

After clearing away the dinner dishes, they usually walked Whiskey together, but Harmony said she had to check something out, and she'd take care of it while he walked the dog. Ry figured it had to do with her day, and he hoped she wouldn't keep him in suspense much longer.

When he returned, she was sitting on the couch with her legs pulled up, waiting for him. There was some paperwork, a beer, and her water bottle on the coffee table. She'd even made a bowl of popcorn for Whiskey.

Something was up, and he didn't think he'd be happy about it.

"Just let me change and we'll talk, okay?" Ry asked. Less than five minutes later, he returned in sweat shorts and a T-shirt, his version of her yoga pants and T-shirt.

Harmony left the television off and was tossing popcorn at Whiskey and giggling as he ran around catching it. Ry shook his head at their antics as he sat on the couch and pulled her into his lap. She tensed. For a moment, he wondered if she'd get up, but she settled against his chest.

"So what's going on, sweetheart? You've got me worried." Ry asked, keeping his voice calm even though his insides were churning.

"It's probably nothing, but you know how you always say you trust your gut? Mine is telling me something is up."

"If something's going on, we'll figure it out together. Remember, you're not alone anymore." Ry reminded her.

Harmony nodded, then kissed his chin. It was so cute and eased some of his tension. "It's been very boring at work, so when Wendy called me into her office just before closing, I was pretty surprised."

"Has she ever done that before?"

"Nope. And what's weirder is she came to my office and stood in the doorway to ask me to come to her office. Weird, right?"

Ry nodded.

"When I went into her office, she made me wait while she finished a call. That was weird too, because she just asked me to come in and I didn't hear her phone ring. But anyway, she put a written warning in my employee file."

Ry tensed, and when she looked up at him, he forced himself to relax. "For what?"

"That's what I asked. The only thing I could think of

would be the trouble with Harry. But it wasn't that, it was for fraternization on bank properly. The goodbye kiss you gave me the day everything went to crap? Apparently, the surveillance camera caught our kiss."

"You got a written warning for that? It was hardly anything and so quick if you sneezed you'd have missed it."

"Exactly. But it wouldn't do any good to argue with her. She told me it was in my employee contract." Harmony picked a document off the table and handed it to him. "She's right, it's there, but I hardly believe they meant a goodbye kiss."

"I doubt it either," Ry said as he perused the contract.

"Then she told me that if it happened again, I'd be terminated. But that wasn't the weird thing. She said I should keep you away from the bank. And implied that if the Harry issue caused trouble in the bank, they'd blame me for it."

"What the fuck?"

"Exactly what I thought, though not in those words." Harmony gave him a half-grin.

She'd come a long way while they were together. The other day, this would have turned her into a huge ball of anxiety.

"I don't get why she told you that I need to stay away. Or why she had to have the discussion in her office. It's almost as if she had someone listening. Is that possible?"

"Maybe? It's possible I suppose. I didn't see if she disconnected the phone call. She could have put it on speaker. Then when she finished talking to me, she picked it up again. She could have just been making another call."

Ry had a bad feeling about all of it, and his neck tingled. Another hunch kicked him in the gut, and it seemed way too plausible. He needed to talk to Chrissy and the guys.

"What are you thinking," Harmony asked.

"I think something else is going on here. I don't know what, but I'm going to figure it out. Until then, just be careful, okay?

"Yup, I will. Does this mean I have spidey sense, too?" She asked and batted her eyelashes at him.

"Yes, it does, baby, most definitely." Ry leaned down and rubbed his lips against hers until she parted for him. His tongue swept inside her mouth, making love to her mouth the way he'd eventually make love to every inch of her.

Moaning, Harmony dug her fingernails into his shoulders as she clung to him. When he finally released her, they were both breathing heavily.

"I love when you do that," she admitted and ducked her head against his shoulder.

"I do too. It's getting harder and harder to stop."

"Maybe we should keep going then," she said shyly.

"Don't tempt me, it would be so easy to carry you to bed and not let you out until all the neighbors hear you scream my name." Ry dreamed about taking her every night, and his morning showers had been more about relief from his constant erection than getting clean.

"Oh, wow."

"Yes, it would definitely be wow. There will be no wow tonight, I'm afraid. I need to make some phone calls to see if we can figure out what's going on. I also have some sad news."

"Oh, no. What's wrong?"

"Barb Ericson passed away the other day. Detective Nelson found out this afternoon."

Harmony's eyes filled with tears. "She was so sweet. I

prayed for her so much. I hoped they'd be able to save her. Poor Harry. He must be devastated."

"No one can find him. I hope he didn't do something stupid."

"Like torch my car?"

He knew she didn't believe he'd done it, and Ry had his doubts as well. But he still was the best suspect they had. "Maybe. Grief does things to people, changes them."

"Maybe, but I just don't think he'd hurt anyone or anything. You didn't see him when they came in the first time. They walked in holding hands. I'd never seen a couple so in love before, and they'd been married for thirty years."

Ry nodded. He wouldn't tell her his doubts, or that he had a feeling her father was in Virginia Beach, until he had proof.

He put the Bourne Identity movie on for Harmony and went into his room to make his calls. First one was to Chrissy. He told her his suspicions, and she said she'd check it out. Then he called Quinn and Josh. He'd found proof that someone was watching his apartment but hadn't been able to catch them.

When Chrissy let him know earlier that William Taylor's phone hadn't left Norwalk, but no one had seen him in a week, Ry's gut had said, 'I told you so,' and he wanted to kick himself for not following up more quickly.

Taylor was dirty through and through, and the guy he'd bribed to marry Harmony was a lawyer in the firm Taylor used for all his legal activities—probably illegal ones too.

If Jim hadn't run away with his secretary, he'd have been under Taylor's thumb, just like Harmony. The last thing Chrissy had uncovered bothered him the most. There had been no sign of her mother for over twenty-five years. The last time anyone had seen her, or she'd used a credit card or anything else, was in Norwalk in March of nineteen-ninety-six.

Once she found him, they'd set the trap and hopefully catch the spider in his own web.

14

Ry had debated whether to tell Harmony about the plan he and Josh had come up with, but after talking to Chrissy too, they decided it was safer if she didn't know. Ry worried it would backfire, but after he'd dropped her off at the bank, it was too late to reconsider.

"Josh, you in position?" Ry asked through his comms. They'd spoken to Quinn last night too, and he gave them permission to 'borrow" the units for testing. As long as they didn't interfere with law enforcement, they would be okay.

"Copy. That bank has lousy security. I set the listening device in Harmony's office like we'd planned. No one stopped me or even asked what I was doing there," Josh said. He was in position behind the bank, watching the rear entrance.

Chrissy's superpowers worked out the plan. After she'd figured out that Wendy was involved, it all fell into place. Then suggested they plant the bug in Harmony's office so they'd hear as well as see what was going on.

Ry hid across the street in an empty storefront, watching with his binoculars. Whiskey was alert and by his side, picking up on his tension. He was so thankful that the front of the bank was all glass. It made it possible for him to easily keep an eye on Harmony and Wendy, and anyone who entered through the front.

"Now we wait for the motherfucker," Ry said, never taking his focus off the front of the bank.

"The calvary just showed up," Josh said.

"Who?"

"All of them," the rest of the team answered.

"I figured you could use the help," Quinn said. "Just tell us where you want us."

Ry swallowed hard. He didn't know what he'd do without his team. "Take as many angles around the bank as we can cover. I don't know how much Daddy Douchebag knows about me, so we need to stay out of view."

"Copy that," they answered one by one.

Quinn came into view a moment later and ducked inside with Ry. "I'll help you cover the front."

"Thanks, boss. I appreciate this."

"I know, but you're gonna have to thank Tony later. He authorized our time off."

"Seriously? Fuck, I'm going to owe him a bottle of scotch for this."

Quinn chuckled. "At least one."

A few hours passed as they waited, but they were used to surveillance. Ry called Harmony at lunchtime like he usually did.

"Hey, sweetheart, how's your day going?" Ry asked, watching her from across the street. It squeezed his heart when he saw her excited smile when she saw it was him calling.

"I'm okay, another boring day in bankland. How about you? Are you having a good one?"

"Eh, it's okay, just a lot of training like usual. Are you going out for lunch today?"

"No, I stole one of your protein bars this morning. I didn't feel like it. My spidey senses are tingling on high today."

"Probably good you're staying inside. I talked to Detective Nelson, still nothing on Harry. So you're probably okay, but it doesn't hurt to be careful. Always trust your gut."

"Yeah, that's what my smart, sexy boyfriend keeps telling me. I should probably listen to him." Harmony giggled.

"He sounds like a really smart guy. I'd definitely listen. Quinn's calling me, I've got to get going. I'll see you at pickup time."

"Okay, have a good afternoon, sweetie."

It wasn't until Ry hung up that he realized she'd called him sweetie. It was the first time, and he wanted to cheer. But then Harry Ericson walked into the bank.

"Is that Ericson?" Quinn asked.

"Yeah, it is. Fuck me running."

"What do you want to do? I'd suggest not calling the cops; they'll go in there guns blazing and we'll never catch what did you call him? Oh yeah, Daddy Douchebag."

"You're right. Let's see what he does." Then he turned on his comms. "Ericson is in the bank. Stay vigilant."

Everyone responded with, "Good copy."

Ry was ready to charge across the street if Ericson so much as leaned toward his woman.

"It'll be okay. Nothing will happen to her," Quinn said.

"That's for fucking sure. I'll rip him apart if he tries anything," Ry threatened.

"But we agreed it's Taylor, right?"

"Yeah, but I still don't trust this guy."

"Got it. There are five SEALs surrounding that bank. Anyone will have to go through us, and you know that doesn't happen."

"Truth. I appreciate it, boss. I wouldn't have been able to do this alone."

"You're never alone, you know that. We're family. Harmony is too, so shut the fuck up and concentrate on her."

"Copy that, boss." Ry grinned, but there was no humor in it. From the way his neck itched, it was only a matter of time before something happened.

The last person Harmony expected to show up at the bank was Harry Ericson. Yet, there he was. He looked nothing like the man she'd met three months earlier when he'd first come in with his wife. The man looked haggard, had a scruffy beard, and messy hair, but it was definitely Harry.

At first, she thought about calling Ry, but she still didn't believe Harry was a threat to her or anyone else.

"Hi, Harry. How are you?"

"Can I come in?" He asked from the doorway.

"Of course." Then she reached behind her to grab a bottle of water and handed it to him. "Are you okay?"

"My Barb died," he said, his voice barely above a whisper.

She'd strained to hear him, but she knew what he'd said.

Tears coursed down his cheeks. He looked so broken.

"I'm so very sorry." Her heart ached for him, and without thinking, she came around the desk and hugged him, all the while thinking it was a good thing Ry couldn't see her; he'd have heart failure.

Harry hugged her back, holding tight and sobbing on her shoulder. He was so broken, and she didn't know what to do for him.

"I'm sorry I threatened you. You've been nothing but kind to us. I hope you know I'd never hurt you," he said as he released her and wiped his tears with his shirtsleeve.

Harmony reached across her desk for a box of tissues and put it in front of him. "I know that. You were just hurt and scared. If I'd had any idea this would happen, I'd never have suggested you take the loan."

"I know. And now that I've lost my Barb, it doesn't matter. I have nothing left to live for. She was my life."

Tears filled Harmony's eyes and her heart squeezed so tightly in her chest she had trouble breathing. His pain was palpable and devastating. "Barb wouldn't want you to give up. Promise me you won't do anything silly. I'll help you, I promise." Even as she said the words, she knew it was her vow. She would do everything she could to make sure he landed on his feet. She wasn't sure how, but she'd make it happen.

"Don't make promises you can't keep, daughter."

The blood drained out of her face, and dizziness almost knocked her over as she stood up from comforting Harry.

He'd found her.

She'd expected him to show up, eventually. Just like she knew he'd been the one to torch her car, or he'd hired someone to do it for him.

"Father, you're a long way from home. How did you find me?" Harmony asked, trying to keep her voice calm. She wasn't in Norwalk, he didn't have help this time.

Harmony leaned against her desk for support and met her father's menacing gaze.

"Awful brave now that you're not at home. Don't worry, I'll fix that fast enough." He grinned when he watched her reach for the edge of her desk.

"I'm not going back. I'm *never* going back."

"Oh, but you are. You have nothing left here. No job, no car, no apartment, nothing."

"You're wrong, I have friends—"

"You won't have them for long. If you think they can do anything to stop me, you've lost your fucking mind. And sleeping with that SEAL? I always knew you were a slut, a whore, just like your mother."

Harmony gripped the edge of her desk until her knuckles turned bright white. Her stomach turned over and she gulped air, trying to keep her stomach contents where they belonged.

"I should have known you drove Mom away. I just wish she'd taken me with her."

"Trust me, you don't. You wouldn't like where she ended up. Now grab whatever you need and we're leaving."

"No, father. I'm not going. I have a life here. And I have a job and an apartment. I'll get a replacement for the car you destroyed. Yeah, I figured that out. But what I don't understand is why you hate me so much, and why you need to control me."

"How can you treat your daughter like this? She's one of the sweetest people I know," Harry said as he listened to their conversation.

"This doesn't concern you, old man. Get the fuck out," Taylor said, as he reached behind his back and pulled out a gun, pointing it at Harmony's chest.

"You're crazy. You can't drag me out of here at

gunpoint. My boss won't let you, neither will the security guard."

"Have you looked around? Do you see anyone coming to your aid? Your boss has been feeding me updates since you started here. I know everything and she runs this bank. The guard won't do a thing. Wendy told them all that you escaped from a mental hospital, and I'm here to take you back."

"What? None of that is true," Harmony exclaimed. Her hope that she'd get out of this dwindled by the moment. Why hadn't she told Ry she loved him? Now she might never get the chance.

"It will be true. I'll keep you locked up for the rest of your life."

"You're an evil man. How can you be my flesh and blood?"

Before he could answer, there was a commotion and the front and back doors of the bank. Ry and his teammates were rushing toward her. Her hero saved her.

"He won't be in time," Taylor said as he leveled the gun.

Then everything moved in slow motion. Ry was screaming for him to drop his weapon as he ran for her. But it didn't stop him. He leveled the gun and pulled the trigger as Harmony closed her eyes, tears streaming down her cheeks. Her heart was already broken for what she wouldn't ever have with Ry.

But there was no pain. She opened her eyes and Harry was on the floor at her feet, blood blossoming across his chest.

"Oh my God, what have you done?" she cried as she kneeled at Harry's side and applied pressure to his chest. "Someone call nine-one-one."

Ry burst into her office and took out her father with

one punch to his jaw, then kicked his gun to the side while Josh dragged him out of the office.

"Are you okay, baby? You're not hurt, are you? I'm so sorry I didn't get here sooner. But I didn't see him pull the gun until it was too late," he said, his voice unsteady.

"It's okay, you're here, and you saved me. He would have killed me or dragged me out of here and no one would have been able to find me. I can't believe he shot Harry."

"The ambulance is already on the way. I'll be okay, I promise."

Harmony nodded through her tears. She'd never forgive herself if Harry died because of her.

The police and ambulance arrived moments later. The paramedics put him on a gurney and rushed him off to the hospital.

Detective Nelson showed up shortly after the patrol cars. He took her father and her boss into custody, although Ry wasn't sure they'd be able to charge her with anything illegal. Unless taking payoffs was enough. After they wheeled Harry out, Ry grabbed the bug from under Harmony's desk, and then handed the detective a flash drive. Everything her father had said was on that drive. Though Harmony wasn't sure if it would be admissible in court, especially if her father got a good lawyer.

"I wish you'd let me in on your little mission," Detective Nelson said as Ry handed him the recording.

"It came together late last night and honestly, we weren't sure it would happen or not. We were acting on a hunch," Ry said. "We got lucky."

"Sure looks like it. I'm happy to know that Mr. Ericson wasn't involved in any way. I hope he pulls through."

Harmony sniffled. Harry's blood covered her hands. So much blood. She didn't know how he'd survive, and she'd never be able to thank him. "I hope so, too. I knew he wouldn't hurt me, and in the end, he helped save me."

Ry put his arm around her and pulled her close.

After what felt like forever, Detective Nelson let them go with the promise that they'd be at the station in the morning to give their official statements.

"I need to go to the restroom and wash off this blood," she murmured as Ry led her out of her office.

"Go ahead, I'll wait right here. Josh grabbed your purse for you. Do you have your phone with you? He couldn't find it."

"Okay," she didn't really hear what he said. All she could focus on was the blood and reliving the moment. It happened so fast. Harry must have dodged in front of her when she'd closed her eyes.

Harmony didn't know how long she stood at the sink, scrubbing her hands to remove Harry's blood, with tears streaming down her cheeks. As she caught her reflection in the mirror, she barely recognized herself. The pale face didn't look anything like her, like someone had drained her life force. Nothing would ever be the same again.

15

A *few days later...*

Fall had arrived in Virginia. Harmony sipped her coffee as she stood on Ry's balcony, admiring the colors of the leaves. It was her first fall on the East Coast, the first of a lot of things.

Last night she'd woken up three times because of the nightmares. Ironically, they weren't about her father. Instead, she'd woken up crying for Harry. Ry told her they'd fade over time, and she believed him. She just wished they'd hurry and go away already.

Behind her, the sliding doors opened, and Ry put his arm around her waist. "It's nice out here, isn't it?"

"It really is. I can't wait to watch the colors turn."

"I'm sure the leaves turned in Iowa," Ry commented.

"Sure they did, but nothing was pretty there. It was all just gray, at least to me."

She saw Ry nod and was thankful that he 'got it' and

she didn't have to explain. She'd done enough explaining to last her a lifetime. Too bad she still didn't know why her father had treated her with such hatred and malice.

"Do you think you're up for some company?" Ry asked, then took a sip of his coffee.

"Sure. I'm not broken, just a little dented," she said. It was true, too. After everything she'd been through, she was stronger now than ever and she owed a lot of that to Ry. Though some of it was her finally realizing that she was a lot stronger than she knew, and it was kind of funny. Since the police had arrested her father, she'd been a lot less klutzy. *Go figure.*

"Good. Chrissy and Ryan are coming. Maybe Josh, too. I think she'll be able to answer a lot of the questions you have."

"Really? That would be a relief. When are they coming?"

Whiskey barked, and a moment later, the doorbell rang.

"Umm, now?" Ry said with a grin.

"Well okay, then. Good thing I'm dressed."

"Chrissy called, and I said it would be okay if they came over now. She might have to leave this afternoon and she didn't want to go without talking to you first."

"It's okay. I want to hear what she has to say. Did she tell you yet?"

"I knew a little about your father, but nope. I don't know what she's found."

"I know you're probably worried, but I lived with him my entire life until four months ago, and I know what he's capable of. There isn't much she can tell me I haven't suspected, anyway. I'll handle it even if I'm not happy about it. I've got this. You taught me that."

Ry smiled and leaned down to kiss her when the doorbell rang again.

"I guess I need to get that." He chuckled.

After one last look at the trees, Harmony followed him inside.

"I'm so glad you're okay," Chrissy said as she hugged Harmony. "I hated we had to keep you in the dark about the plan. But we didn't even know if he'd show up."

"It's okay. Ry explained it all, and it was the right thing to do. Besides, no one expected him to have a gun. I should have figured, but I've never seen him with one."

Ryan and Josh followed behind Chrissy. Harmony hugged each of them, giving Josh an extra squeeze. She'd gotten to know him a lot better over the last few days, and she really liked him and his potty mouth.

"Anyone want coffee, or something else?" Harmony asked as they followed Ry into the living room.

"If I have any more coffee, I will probably go supersonic," Chrissy joked.

Josh and Ryan shook their heads.

Ry pulled two chairs over from the island for Josh and Ryan. Chrissy sat in the recliner, leaving the couch for Ry and Harmony. As she scooted next to Ry and he rested his arm along her shoulders, the anxiety that twisted her gut and set her pulse racing eased.

"Before I start, I just want to say that your father is a cocksucker and I hope he rots in jail for the rest of his life."

"Gee, babe, don't hold back," Ryan said to his fiancée.

"I won't," she replied with a smirk. "I'm glad I still have some friends in the FBI, or I'd have had a lot harder time figuring this shit out."

"I'm glad you do, too. And whatever you found is okay, don't worry about telling me."

Chrissy nodded. "Okay. I found out about your mom.

Her name was Lilibeth Monroe before she married your sperm donor. She was the only child of older parents and very wealthy."

A pang of grief squeezed Harmony's heart when she realized Chrissy was using past tense when she referred to her mom.

"From what I could find out, they were happy for a while. The first sign of trouble happened after you turned three. That's when your mom changed her will, leaving everything to you."

"She did? You said her parents were wealthy, but…"

"Oh yeah, a shit ton of it. In fact, you're a multi-millionaire."

"No way."

"Yup, so next round of drinks is on you," Chrissy teased.

"No problem," Harmony replied, trying to wrap her brain around what she'd just learned.

"Anyway, her attorney was in cahoots with your sperm donor and told him about the will. Apparently, your father flipped out. Shortly after that, your mom disappeared. We now know that she was killed, but not whether it was an accident or on purpose."

Harmony's eyes filled with tears for the woman she barely remembered. There would never be a reunion, and she hadn't deserted her. It was all on her father. "And no one knew or did anything about it?"

"Oh, people knew, they just kept their mouths shut. The lawyer and the sheriff helped him pull it off. That's how we know a lot of this now. Sheriff Donovan agreed to testify against your father for a reduced sentence. That's how the FBI found your mother's body this morning. They'll release her body to you after they complete the investigation. I'm so sorry, Harmony. I really wish I'd been able to find her alive."

Harmony wished it too, but it wasn't Chrissy's fault. It was her father's fault.

"The people in Norwalk, Iowa had quite the shock this morning when the FBI rolled in, I'm sure. They arrested not only Larry Witt, your mom's attorney, but Sheriff Donovan too. Since your father was mayor, they're really fucked now."

"Oh, wow. I didn't even think about that," Harmony said, wondering how many people had known and did nothing to stop any of it.

"The only reason your old boss, Patrick Henniger, didn't get arrested is because they won't be able to prove he knew about the will. Or that the money should have been going to you after you turned twenty-one."

Harmony nodded. "Is that everything?"

"Yes, well mostly. The FBI is still investigating, so some things can't be discussed. I shouldn't even know, probably. Oh, there is one more thing. You'll be hearing from an attorney from Tanger and Witt soon about your inheritance. At least you won't have to go back to that bank. Just think of all the options open to you now. You deserve it. That fucktard put you through hell."

Harmony agreed, but it was still surreal. She'd been worried about going back to the bank and getting a new car. Now, none of that mattered. She could do like Ry suggested and figure out what made her happy.

"Thank you, Chrissy. I really appreciate that you found all of this out. Without you, my father would probably have gotten away with all of it." She shuddered thinking about spending the rest of her life locked up in a mental institution.

"You're most welcome. I'm glad I could help. It sucks,

but now you can move on. That douchebag won't ever bother you again."

"Hopefully not. But what if they don't convict him?"

"They will. There's more than enough evidence. If they could prove he killed your mom deliberately, he could get the death penalty."

"I can't say I'd be sorry if it happened," Josh said, and Ryan nodded in agreement.

"Me, either," Ry said.

Harmony didn't know what to think. She was sure she'd loved him at some point, but now all she could think about was that he'd shot Harry and wanted to lock her up. Maybe him being locked up would be enough.

"If I find out anything else I can share, I'll let you know. But I need to get going. I'm probably going to disappear for a few weeks," Chrissy said.

Harmony knew Ryan hated when she went on missions, but it was the same for Chrissy when Ryan went on missions.

"You need a guys' night, Ryan, so you're not sad when Chrissy's away," Harmony suggested.

Chrissy laughed. But Ryan nodded. "That might not be a bad idea, actually. Take care. If you need anything, let us know," Ryan added as they headed for the door.

The apartment seemed almost too full while Chrissy shared her findings, but after they'd left, it seemed empty and too quiet. Even sitting snuggled between Ry and Whiskey, Harmony shivered.

Ry tipped up her chin, so she'd look at him. "It'll be okay, sweetheart. Remember, you're not alone. You have me and a whole new family who care about you. Just take it one day at a time."

For the first time in her life, she really believed that everything would be okay.

The trust in Harmony's eyes almost brought Ry to his knees.

"After all you've been through, your trust humbles me," he murmured. His lips rubbed against hers, waiting for her to accept him. As they parted, his tongue swept inside and rubbed against hers, possessing her mouth the way he wanted to have all of her.

Needing more of her, Ry pulled her onto his lap and helped her straddle him, her knees on either side of his hips. He groaned as her core pressed against his throbbing cock, as it painfully pushed against his zipper. And still, it wasn't enough. He needed to be inside her until he didn't know where he ended, and she began.

Harmony's hands slid around his neck, her nails scraping along his scalp. Their tongues tangled and rubbed against each other. She was driving him out of his mind with need.

When he finally released her lips, they were both panting. He wrapped his arms around her shoulders. Then he tucked her head under his chin as he struggled to control his need to make her his.

"I'm barely hanging on to my control here," Ry said, his voice gruff.

"Then let go, Ry. I know you've been holding back, but you don't have to."

"Baby, I need to know if you're still a virgin." Ry had his suspicions, but he needed to know before he went any further.

Harmony stilled in his arms, then nodded. "I am, but it doesn't matter. I love you, Ry. I want to know what it's like to be loved by you—all of you."

Ry leaned back so he could see her face, read her

expression. Wanted to spend the rest of his life doing all the things she'd said, and more, but he had to be sure she wouldn't have regrets. He'd never been with a virgin, and it scared him. Worried him. Could he be gentle enough? He wanted to give her the fairytale and make it perfect. She'd suffered so much, he wanted to give her the happily ever after she deserved.

"Are you sure, sweetheart? I'll be gentle, it is going to hurt, but hopefully not for long."

Harmony caressed his cheek, and her beautiful smile lit her entire face and eased his doubts.

"I love you, Harmony." Ry stood with her still in his arms and carried her into his bedroom. Whiskey had followed them down the hall. "Sorry, boy, we need some alone time." Then kicked the door closed.

Harmony giggled. "I can't believe you locked him out."

"Trust me, you do not want him jumping on the bed. Besides, we'd scar him for life." Ry grinned, then kissed her on the tip of her nose before sitting her on the edge of his bed.

He went down on his knees, his hands resting on her thighs. "We're going to take this slow, but if you change your mind at any point, tell me and I'll stop. This is all about you. Showing you how much I love you. But if it doesn't happen today, then it will happen tomorrow, or the next day. No matter what, I'm not going anywhere. You are mine." Ry's gaze never left hers, hoping she would see the truth in his words. He'd wait a hundred years if that's what she needed.

"I'm sure. I have been, but I didn't know if you wanted me…" her voice trailed off as her cheeks turned pink.

She was precious.

"I will always want you." Ry stood and pulled his T-shirt over his head and tossed it on the chair in the corner.

Then he opened the button on his fly and slowly lowered the zipper. His cock was hard enough to hammer nails as it bounced against his stomach as he stepped out of his jeans.

"Oh wow, um, you're kind of big," Harmony murmured as she watched him undress.

"Yes, I am." Before he could say anything else, she tentatively reached out and touched the tip with her finger, then continued down the length of his shaft.

"It's so soft and hard at the same time."

Ry groaned. He wanted her to be comfortable, but it was taking every bit of his restraint to remain still while she explored. When she wrapped her small hand around him and squeezed, he had to stop her.

"I love you want to touch me, and I'll let you explore all you want later, but now it's my turn." He tried to keep his voice gentle but vibrated with the need for her.

"I'm sorry—"

"You have nothing to be sorry about. I want to take this slow and if you keep touching me, I won't be able to."

"Oh."

He'd intended the kiss to be gentle, to distract her as he undressed her, but as soon as their lips touched, he couldn't hold back his desire. Slanting his mouth against hers, he nibbled her bottom lip, and she moaned. Ry pushed her yoga pants down her legs, and she kicked them off. Releasing her lips, he lifted her T-shirt over her head, and it joined his on the chair. Then he stood back and admired his woman.

"You're absolutely beautiful."

"You might need some glasses. I'm pretty normal," she said, as her blush spread over the pale skin of her chest. "I don't even have sexy lingerie—"

"You are exceptional and mine. I don't care about your underwear. You won't be wearing it for much longer." The time for talking was over. Ry climbed onto the bed and pulled her into the middle.

After taking possession of her mouth, he kissed across her jaw and down her neck, learning what she liked. Her nipples were hard and poked against the white cotton of her bra. As his mouth covered the firm nub, Harmony's back arched off the bed.

"Oh my God."

Ry licked and sucked the hard nub through the fabric while he teased the other with his fingers, rubbing back and forth as she shuddered beneath him. Then he switched to the other breast. Reaching behind her back, he unhooked her bra and slid it off her shoulders, and he licked his lips in anticipation.

So soft. So perfect. And all his. Sucking her nipple into his mouth, he rubbed his tongue over it as he held it gently between his teeth.

"Oh my God, Ry, that feels so good. Don't stop," she begged.

Ry chuckled. He had no intention of stopping and took his time with each breast, licking and teasing her nipples. Then he continued down her stomach, kissing and licking until he reached her panties, then slid them down her legs.

His cock ached with the need to be inside her, but when he had his first glimpse of her pink pussy, glistening with her juices, he needed to taste her. Moving between her thighs, he licked her thigh.

"What are you doing?"

"I'm tasting your juices, and they're delicious," Ry said with a smile.

"But that's not—"

Ry licked along her pussy lips, and she dropped onto the pillow with a low moan. He licked up her juices, then rubbed his tongue over her clit. Her hips arched off the bed as she screamed his name.

"Oh my God, oh my God. That was oh amazing," Harmony said.

"We're just beginning, sweetheart," Ry answered, then continued to lick her clit as he slid one finger into her hot pussy.

Fuck. She was so tight. Worry that he'd hurt her shook him to his core. He licked and sucked on her clit, working his finger in and out of her tight pussy. Then he added a second finger, pumping in and out and making sure he hit her G-spot.

As her muscles clenched his fingers, she came for the second time, and his cock throbbed in response.

Grabbing a condom from the bedside table, he slid over her. Then kissed her until she settled.

"I love you, sweetheart. Are you ready for me?" He'd done all he could to ease the way, but it would hurt. She was just too tight for it not to.

"Yes, definitely yes." Her smile wrapped him in sunshine.

"It will hurt, and I'm sorry, but then it will feel amazing."

"I trust you, Ry. I want this, I want you."

As his lips took hers again, he thrust inside her. She cried out in pain and tightened around him. It took everything he had to remain still until she relaxed. "Are you okay, baby?"

"Yes, I am. It did hurt, but it's better now."

Ry kissed her again, then slowly eased out and back in. Watching her expression for signs of pain, he moved slowly at first. When her hips lifted to meet his, he pumped faster until he found the rhythm he needed.

The walls of her pussy tightened as she screamed. The

force of her orgasm pushed him over the edge, coming so hard he saw stars.

Ry took a moment to catch his breath, then went to the bathroom to get rid of the condom. When he came back to bed, he pulled her against his side and kissed her.

"I hope I didn't hurt you too badly."

"When can we do it again?" She asked, as she caressed his chest.

Ry burst out laughing. "I think I need some recovery time, and you're going to be sore."

"I don't care. You, it, wow. I finally understand what they meant in my romance books. Thank you for showing me the stars, Ry. I love you."

Ry didn't know how he'd gotten so lucky, but when he'd found her, he'd found his forever. "And I love you, sweetheart."

16

One month later…

Harmony was practically bouncing up and down in the passenger seat. Her excitement was contagious, and Ry couldn't wipe the smile off his face. Harmony had been waiting for this day for weeks, and yesterday the call came.

"Do you think he'll be excited?" she asked again.

"You'll know soon enough," he replied as they drove across town.

"Oh my gosh, you're such a brat."

Ry grinned. He couldn't believe how much she'd changed over the last two months. Harmony had finally blossomed into the woman she should have been. The changes hadn't been easy for her, especially when she found out the truth about her mother's disappearance.

"I'm driving as fast as I can. I promise. You see all this traffic, right?"

"Yes. I don't mean to be a nag, but I can't wait."

"I know, sweetheart. I can't either. Today is going to be a very special day," Ry said. Looking over to see Harmony's beautiful smile, it was weird not having to look through his dog. The truck seemed a lot larger without Whiskey shoved between them, but today they'd have an extra passenger, so Whiskey had to stay home.

Ry pulled into the parking lot, and Harmony cheered.

"Yay. We're finally here."

He went around the truck to open her door and help her out.

After stopping at the nurses' station, they went into his room.

"Hi Harry," Harmony said.

He was sitting in a chair next to the bed. Harmony said he looked like he did when she'd first met him. Ry was just happy that he'd pulled through.

"Harmony, Ry, how are you? I'm so happy to see you."

"We're doing great, you're the one recovering from the bullet wound."

"Eh, the doctor said it didn't hit anything major, and it's helped me lose a few pounds," he teased.

"That's not true, and you know it. My stomach twists in knots when I think about how you looked lying on the floor. There was so much blood."

"You need to let it go, sweetie. I'm fine now. And that guy who didn't deserve to be your father is getting what's coming to him. Right?"

"Yes, but I almost didn't get the chance to thank you for saving me," Harmony said as she took his hand and kneeled down next to him.

"I didn't save you. I just took a step to the left at the right time. I think this fella here is the real hero."

Ry grinned. He may have helped, but it was Harry

who took a bullet for his woman, and he'd never forget the debt he owed him.

"Anyway, enough mushy stuff. It looks like I might get out next week. Want to help me find an apartment?"

"There's been a slight change in plans, Harry. You're getting released today, and we already found you a place to live," Harmony said. Her smile lit her face with sunshine and filled his heart with happiness. Harry wasn't the only one getting a surprise.

"Do you need help with your clothes?" Ry asked as Harmony unpacked the clothing they'd brought for him.

"I think I can get it. I better if they're tossing me out on my butt," Harry said with a grin. "You'll have to step outside, young lady."

"Yes, sir." Harmony winked at Ry and stepped into the hallway.

"You're lucky to have that girl, you'd better treat her right," Harry said as he buttoned his shirt.

"I know just how lucky I am. Harmony stole my heart when she almost took out a wedding cake," Ry said, grinning at the memory.

"I bet that's a funny story." Harry chuckled and pulled up his pants.

"Ask her. I'm sure she'll tell you," Ry said. He opened the door to let Harmony back in.

"All ready, Harry?" Harmony asked.

"Don't I need to sign some things, pay a bill or two, something?" Harry asked.

"I think the police department covered it for taking down a dangerous criminal, or maybe it was the bank. I don't remember. It's taken care of. That's all that matters," Harmony said.

Ry wondered how long it would take for Harry to put two and two together and come up with Harmony.

"I suppose so. Can't blame me for wondering. I haven't had the best of luck lately."

Hearing Harry's comment as he brought in the wheelchair from the hallway, Ry chuckled. "I think your luck might be changing."

They finally got Harry out of the hospital and into his truck. He chattered the entire drive about the nurses and how different life was without Barb. Then he grew quiet, and his eyes opened wide as they pulled into the driveway of the house he and Barb had lived in. Ry kept calling it the house that started it all, but Harmony thought he was just too silly.

"Why are we here?" Harry asked, his voice barely above a whisper.

"We told you we were driving you home," Harmony said gently.

"But the bank foreclosed. Didn't they?"

"Yes, but I bought it for you. This way, you'll always have Barb with you. I remember how you talked about this place the first time I met you. I couldn't let you lose it."

"I can't accept this, it's too much—" Harry said as he stared out the windshield at the house he'd called home for the last thirty years.

"Listen, I have way more money than I will ever need. Please let me help you. If it weren't for my suggestion, you'd never have gotten into trouble."

"That's not true. I would have done anything to save my Barb."

"Yes, and now you're our family," Harmony said with a smile. "And families stick together no matter what. I want you to always be a part of my life. C'mon, it's time to go home."

"You're amazing. I can't thank you enough. Barb

would be so thankful, too. I'm sure she's looking down on you and smiling."

Harmony hugged Harry before Ry helped him out of the truck. "I'm sure she's smiling down on all of us."

Ry wrapped his arms around Harmony's waist and lifted her out of the truck, hugging her closely before setting her down. "Sweetheart, you're one of the kindest, most loving people I've ever met. Wonderful from the top of your blonde head to the bottom of your cute little feet. Never forget that."

Harmony shook her head. "I'm just a normal person. You're the amazing one."

He'd planned on waiting until they were alone, for the perfect moment. As Ry gazed into Harmony's face, he knew in his heart that this was that moment.

"But I can't sing and I'm a total klutz—"

"None of that matters," Ry said. He put his hand over her heart. "This right here is all that matters." Then he dropped on one knee and pulled out a ring box from his pocket. "I love you, Harmony Taylor. Will you take my name and be my forever?"

As soon as he said the words, he opened the box, and her eyes went wide in surprise. Ry had searched for weeks for the ring. When he'd seen the oval diamond encircled by amethysts the color of her eyes, he knew he'd found it.

Ry had a moment of panic when she didn't immediately say yes. But a heartbeat later, she kneeled in front of him and laid her hand against his cheek and smiled, her love for him shining in her violet eyes.

"Yes, yes, a thousand times, yes. From the time I was little, I dreamed about a hero coming to my rescue. Then you walked into my life and were the answer to all my dreams. I'd be honored to spend forever with you."

Overwhelmed with emotion, Ry lifted Harmony into

his arms and spun her around as she laughed with glee. Her joy was infectious, and he and Harry joined in. Then he set her down and claimed her with a kiss until he could have her all to himself and show her just how wonderful forever would be.

EPILOGUE

Three months later…

"Where the fuck is Josh?" Quinn asked as he checked his watch for the second time in the last few minutes.

They were all sitting around the conference table, waiting for a briefing. Everyone but Josh. Last evening, Quinn had texted each of them to let them know they needed to be on base at zero seven hundred for a briefing. As usual, they were in the dark, though Ry suspected Quinn knew what they'd be discussing.

If Ry had to guess, he'd say it was about shit happening in Marikistan. For the last few months, he'd been following their civil war. It had escalated over the last week and the UN sent aid workers. Then again, it wasn't the only trouble spot in the news these days.

"I called to check on him. He's on his way. He said his

neighbor blocked his driveway again so he couldn't avoid her," Ry said.

Hopefully, Josh showed up before their CO, Tony Knox. Though Quinn was so pissed off, he'd probably still make him do extra PT for the rest of the week.

None of the team had met Josh's next-door neighbor, but from his stories, they knew plenty about her. Or at least how much of a pain in the ass she was. From the moment she moved in, she'd been driving Josh out of his mind over the stupidest little things, but this time she'd gone too far. You didn't make a SEAL late for a briefing. That was a hell fucking no.

"I'm here. Sorry, boss," Josh said as he rushed through the door and took a seat next to Ry. "It won't happen again."

Quinn wasn't usually a hardass, but something was eating him. It didn't bode well for Josh or whatever the briefing was about.

Josh had barely sat down before Knox entered, and he wasn't alone. A woman followed behind him, talking into her phone. He'd never seen her before and from the low murmur between his teammates, neither had they.

She had thick black hair that fell to the middle of her back, and fair skin. But when she disconnected her call, and she looked up, he couldn't look away. He'd never seen eyes so pale blue they looked like ice on a cold winter's day, and he actually shivered. No way would he want to be on the wrong side of her ire.

"Oh, fuck no," Josh exclaimed, loud enough for everyone to hear.

Shocked at his outburst, Ry glanced over at Josh and gave him a look that said, "What the fuck?"

"Good morning. Sorry to make this so early, but we have a situation. Before I begin, I'd like to introduce

Tempest Miller. She'll be working with us on this mission as a translator and trainer.

He didn't have to look at him to know Josh was trying to control his temper. Who'd have thought that of all the people in this world, it was the one woman who drove him out of his fucking mind?

Oh yeah, this was going to be fun.

The End

If you enjoyed SEAL's Harmony, I hope you'll consider leaving a review. It's one of the best ways to help an author. Don't forget to preorder *SEAL's Tempest*, Josh and Tempest's enemies-to-lovers story.

ACKNOWLEDGMENTS

Some books are more difficult to write than others, and the first in a series is usually the hardest, at least for me. Before I can begin any story, I have to learn about my characters, and they need to tell me their stories. This book was especially difficult. Maybe it was the characters, or all the health issues in my family, a combination of those, or maybe just 2021.

Whatever the reason, it took a long time, and I had to postpone the release date a few times. I apologize for this. I hated to do it, but it was necessary. And now it's finally here and I hope you enjoy Ry and Harmony's story. It wouldn't have happened without the support of so many people, including my Coffee Crew, and a few people who I am proud to call my friends. I can't thank Trish, Katie, Patti, and Heather enough for all the love and cheerleading, and maybe a few whippings. Thank you also to Rebecca, who jumped in at the last minute and kept my butt out of the fire.

Lynne

xoxo

ABOUT THE AUTHOR

Lynne St. James is an Amazon bestselling author by night and an IT Project Manager by day.

Lynne writes mostly romantic suspense with military heroes and the strong women they fight to protect. But she also has series that are contemporary, new adult, and paranormal. All her books, no matter what the genre, include danger, passion, family, humor, and a happily-ever-after.

Originally from up north, Lynne now makes her home in the mostly sunny state of Florida with her husband, Lulu the Yorkie-poo, and an orange tabby named Pumpkin who thinks he rules them all—and mostly does!

When Lynne's not writing or daydreaming about her next book, she's drinking coffee and reading or crocheting.

Where to find Lynne:

Email: lynne@lynnestjames.com

Amazon: https://amzn.to/2sgdUTe

BookBub: https://www.bookbub.com/authors/lynne-st-james

Facebook: https://www.facebook.com/authorLynneStJames

Website: http://lynnestjames.com

Instagram: https://www.instagram.com/lynnestjames/

Pinterest: https://www.pinterest.com/lynnestjames5

VIP Newsletter sign-up: https://bit.ly/3iX8Tr0

BOOKS BY LYNNE ST. JAMES

Red Falcon Team

SEAL's Harmony, Book 1

SEAL's Tempest, Book 2

Delta 3 Team Collaboration

Gwen's Delta, Book 3

Black Eagle Team

SEAL's Spitfire: Special Forces: Operation Alpha, Book 1

SEAL's Sunshine: Special Forces: Operation Alpha, Book 2

SEAL's Hellion: Special Forces: Operation Alpha, Book 3

SEAL's Sky: Special Forces: Operation Alpha, Book 4

SEAL's Angel: Special Forces: Operation Alpha, Book 5

Beyond Valor

A Soldier's Gift, Book 1

A Soldier's Forever, Book 2

A Soldier's Triumph, Book 3

A Soldier's Protection, Book 4

A Soldier's Pledge, Book 5

A Soldier's Destiny, Book 6

A Soldier's Temptation, Book 7

A Soldier's Homecoming, Book 8 (coming soon)

A Soldier's Redemption, Book 9 (coming Soon)

Raining Chaos

Taming Chaos

Seducing Wrath

Music under the Mistletoe—A Raining Chaos Christmas (Novella)

Tempting Flame

Anamchara

Embracing Her Desires

Embracing Her Surrender

Embracing Her Love

Want to be one of the first to learn about Lynne St. James's new releases? Sign up for her newsletter filled with exclusive VIP news and contests! https://bit.ly/3iX8Tr0

Made in the USA
Las Vegas, NV
25 November 2021

35251726R00111